The tree branches became bone. . . .

Fruits like organs hung from the limbs, purple-pink clumps of smooth flesh. Beads of bloody sap oozed from the trunk, and a thick odor of decay fouled the air.

Sibatia climbed on, higher and higher.

Eventually, he found the skull wedged in a fork, the six black seeds lying snug within.

With the utmost care, while reciting the prescribed litany, he removed them one by one, gently swallowing each in turn, the moist gelatinous orbs shivering against his tongue as he forced them down. The last one gone, he closed his eyes and prayed.

"Is she the one?" a voice asked from above.

Turning, Sibatia saw the city in the distance. And high above the pinnacles of the obelisk and monuments, above the golden minarets and spires, the trestles, aqueducts, and silver-spun bridges arching over the city's streets and parks—in the tallest tower of them all, standing at a window on the uppermost floor, Sibatia saw the American girl, Molly—naked, her belly swollen and ripe, her eyes fixed on his—and *Yes*, he thought, *Yes, she's the one. Yes.* . . .

Dry Skull Dreams

Michael Green

POCKET BOOKS
New York   London   Toronto   Sydney   Tokyo   Singapore

An *Original* Publication of POCKET BOOKS

POCKET BOOKS, a division of Simon & Schuster Inc.
1230 Avenue of the Americas, New York, NY 10020

ISBN: 0-671-89739-X

First Pocket Books printing March 1995

10 9 8 7 6 5 4 3 2 1

POCKET and colophon are registered trademarks of Simon & Schuster Inc.

Cover art by Jim Warren

Printed in the U.S.A.

A baby, wrapped in a yellow and black shawl ... a
sleeping baby, its tiny face lit by Tembro's light.

Whether it happened so or not I do not know, but if you think about it you can see that it is true.

Black Elk

For Jill

PROLOGUE

Red Heaven

There are places in this world where the stars withdraw their shining, where every twenty-eight days the full moon turns to blood.

There are places in this world where the wind cannot be said to spring from any of the thirty-two points. Where the white cities burn, each ignited by its own cold sun.

Where mothers are so frightened, they won't allow their babies to be born.

This grim and grinding world . . . It never lets up.

Plagued by pains of loneliness, their spirits descending to the Deeps, through their own inventions men have become more like beasts every day. Savage of temper, they have slain the one-celled green creatures in the sea, and thus shut off the oxygen. Stripping the planet of its bounty, with their bloody hands they tirelessly work for one another's destruction, until the Earth is wet with mindless slaughter.

Though they are more plentiful than the ants, Mother Death shall seize them all.

1

And for that, we should feel sorry?

Meru shook his head and stooped to pluck a tasty-looking pebble from the path.

The Men of Iron pouring from the dark factories, quarrelsome and ignorant, eating flesh as well as grain. The Plastic Men, degenerate and pitiless, gnawed by lust and knowing no shame . . .

Like the world didn't deserve a little break?

Hey, it should be so lucky.

Pausing to catch his fleeing breath, Meru surveyed the bleak hillside, the desolate landscape of packed red dirt and rock beneath a dim and sunless sky. Not Earth's sky exactly, but some place alien and distant.

Scattered along the path, small black husks like Styrofoam peanuts crackled beneath his sandals, tiny empty corpses strewn upon the dust. The air smelled strongly of ash.

Where were his son's brains? This latest scheme of his . . .

"I cannot allow it," Meru said aloud.

He was dead set against such madness. Just the idea alone brought a harsh taste to his mouth.

To tomorrow Meru had already said good-bye. He was an old dying man, and good riddance, right? But how could he leave such a crazy sonofabitch behind? Who would ever forgive him?

His bastard son.

Enough already . . .

Like he hadn't gone over this ten thousand times before?

Yawing slightly, he started climbing again, bending to scoop up another small stone from along the pathway. Slipping it into his mouth, he cracked it in

2

half between his back teeth, and then in half once more, rolling the pieces across his tongue.

All right, then, so this would be the boy's final chance. Either he showed some signs of sense here, or else.

It was a blessing, thanks God, that his poor mother wasn't alive to witness this.

Mounting the shoulder of the rise at last, Meru turned and glanced around. At the base of the hill, east and west, clouds borne on a gentle wind crowded against the edge of the world. Up above there was only the Big Sky, and in front and behind it was the same. Far below to the south lay an immense mass that might have been heaped-up water. Or blood. Where it had come from, no one recalled.

A wooden table and two chairs waited just ahead.

Where was that fool boy?

Tired from the arduous climb, Meru shuffled over to the table and sat. His breath whistled hollowly in his chest and his heart raced back and forth. Such an old man he'd become, carrying this sorry body of his around, shrunken and frail, this carcass made of parchment and sticks. He could feel his flesh pulling away from his bones, his bones turning brittle and dry. His neck was a thin stem and the strength in his limbs was all but gone.

The fly appeared first, fat and pale, alighting on the table without a sound. Meru instinctively slapped at it with his palm, but the thing was so rubbery it simply shook itself and flew off.

Next came the black dog, bounding into sight, circling the table several times in a mad dash, leaping and snapping at the air hungrily with each pass behind Meru's chair.

3

"Hello, Father," Sibatia said, climbing the rise a moment later.

As bedraggled and unkempt as ever, you'd think he'd spent his entire life sleeping under a bush. Approaching the table, he pulled back the other chair and sat.

"Glad to see me?" he asked. "You look like you could shit yourself with joy."

"Take care with your language," Meru told him, angered. "Why don't you wash yourself sometimes? Why must you always stink like a dog?"

Growling, the black cur skidded to a sudden halt and clamped his jaws firmly around the leg of Meru's chair.

"You keep the talk on a high plane, don't you, Father?" Sibatia chuckled. Kicking the dog beneath the table, he motioned it away. "Enough, Pudzie. Go make dirty. Go on, boy."

Obediently, the dog trotted off and squatted in the dust, his face turned skyward as he strained.

"Listen," Meru began. "Listen to me now."

"I'd rather get a fart out of a dead donkey."

Meru did not answer. What could he possibly say? It was clearly hopeless.

"I withdraw my request for your assistance," Sibatia stated. When he smiled, a white fly danced from between his parted lips.

"The American girl," Meru persisted. "She must be left untouched."

"This is my business now, Father. Attend to yours."

"I have spoken with Uncle," Meru lied. And why not? "I have informed him of your ridiculous scheme. If you so much as sow a single seed, he will know."

Sibatia sat quietly for a moment, absently watching

4

Pudzo struggle at his stool. "You dried-up old puke," he finally said. "I'll pinch your head clean off for that."

He was up and around the table before Meru could react.

His face twisted by a sharp crimson rage, he locked his hands tight around Meru's skull, the insanity leaping out of his yellow-tinged eyes. Hooting softly, he pressed with all his might, and Meru instantly sensed some part of his innermost soul being grasped and shifted.

For a long, hellish moment his body refused to believe the extent of his pain.

"I'll make your bones sing, old man," Sibatia hissed. "Set me as a seal upon your heart."

Calling up his reserves of strength in a desperate effort, Meru lashed out, but too late! Too late! As his son's power flooded into him, his limbs began to violently shudder.

That settles your pickle, he thought.

And just like that, he was way out there, practically at the gates.

"Here we go, huh?" Sibatia said. "Here we go."

What a world . . . It never lets up.

When everything finally went white, he died as quietly as a bird rising in the sky.

PART 1

~

The lovely

CHAPTER ONE

1

Molly Coughlin had certainly had her share of strange dreams while in Africa, but this was by far the strangest. It stayed with her that entire day, her last in the village, haunting her like a lingering shadow, a soft, ghostly caress.

In the dream, she was home again, in the backyard of her parents' house in Brattleboro. At least that's where she thought she was. She recognized the swimming pool and her mother's vegetable garden, but where the toolshed should've been there was a mud hut with a thatched straw roof. And lying in the dirt in front of the hut was a young girl, nine or ten years old.

Except for a small red apron covering her loins, the girl was naked. Her head was shaved, and her body was slick with oil. Staring up at the sky, her face was as expressionless as a mask.

Glancing down at herself, Molly realized that she too was wearing nothing but a red cloth around her waist. Then the door of the hut abruptly creaked open

9

and an old black woman dressed in a dirty white burnoose stepped outside, raising a clawlike hand and gesturing for her to enter.

Walking slowly forward, Molly carefully stepped around the girl on the ground and approached the hut. The woman grinned and nodded to her, and for just an instant Molly paused and looked at her closely. Despite the fact that her skin was dark and most of her teeth were missing, she bore a striking resemblance to Molly's mother.

Turning away, the woman let the door swing shut behind her as she stepped into the hut. Following after her, Molly was shocked to find her father on the floor in the center of the room.

Lying beneath a naked little girl, he was using his arms and legs to hold her down, forcing her legs wide apart. Stripped bare himself, he pressed up against her, rocking her small body as he whispered into her ear.

There were several other girls gathered on a low wooden bench along the far wall, all of them crying quietly. Ribbons of blood curled down their dark legs, pooling on the dusty floor.

Dizzy and breathless, Molly sat down on a chair beside the door.

As she watched, the old woman quickly shuffled forward, removing a knife and a pair of pliers from the pocket of her robe. Squatting down next to the girl, she spat into her palm, then reached out and began massaging the girl's vagina with her fingertips.

Sweet and lilting, she sang a quiet lullaby as Molly's father tightened his grip and moaned.

Leaning forward, the old woman took hold of the girl's flesh with the pliers, the knife flashing down and sawing back and forth, the blood splashing onto the floor. Molly turned away, but not before she saw her father staring up at her, his eyes bright and full of love.

She felt a sharp tingling between her own legs then, and looking down at herself, lifting the red apron and spreading her thighs, Molly saw a column of tiny green lizards pouring out of her as if from a nest, lizards no larger than ants, a steady stream of minuscule creatures marching in single file down the leg of the chair and out of sight.

And then at last it was over—and she was safe in her bed, her mother's soft lullaby lingering in the air for an instant like a foul odor.

The fact that her brain could come up with such a twisted nightmare was embarrassing.

Christ, her *parents?*

All that day, again and again, the images had returned to haunt her. Those poor little girls, already circumcised, sitting inside the hut. Her father's urgent whispering. Her mother's bloody hands.

The lizards coming out of her . . .

Enough.

For the umpteenth time, Molly pushed the dream from her mind.

Her parents?

Sighing, she watched the group of kids playing in the river before her, splashing in the muddy water near shore, laughing and shouting as they wrestled one another over a bright scrap of cloth. On the opposite bank two older boys were fishing with sticks and strings, standing in a patch of shade. Old Mr. Bayma, the village shopkeeper, lounged beneath a tree behind them, his three-legged dog lying nearby.

Lifting her camera, Molly focused on the tumbling

kids in the river, taking a shot of them all piled together, and then another of the two boys fishing. The land stretched away into the distance beyond them, flat and barren, the few scattered trees stark and bent, the dusty brown fields dotted with low leafless shrubs.

For the second consecutive year the wet season had been disastrous, the sky refusing to rain. Everywhere you looked, the land was slowly baking, the grasslands turning brittle and dry, the soil cracked and sere.

Whenever Molly mentioned the drought, people would shake their heads and look down at the ground, scuffing their toes against the powdery soil. The rains will come when it's time for them to come, they'd say. If not this week, then next.

Well, maybe. But then again, maybe not.

"Labass!" Mr. Bayma suddenly hollered to her from across the river. "Hello there, miss."

Returning his wave, Molly held up her camera for him to see, then took his picture, his dog yapping at her for a moment before limping down to the river for a drink, the two boys setting aside their poles and going over to play with him, tossing a stick into the water and coaxing him to chase after it. Taking one final picture—the sunlight dancing in the river where it rippled over the white stones—Molly turned and climbed the bank, leaving the sounds of the laughing kids behind her as she headed back toward the village.

Not all that long ago the river had run swift and deep year-round. After the rains, it would sometimes even rise high enough to flood the surrounding fields. Now old men and three-legged dogs walked across it every day, and no one bothered to fish in it but boys with nothing better to do.

Soon this entire valley, along with the rest of the country, was just going to dry up and blow away.

Feeling uncomfortably like a tourist, Molly paused to take several photographs of the village as she approached it—the red mud houses arranged in labyrinthine clusters, the rooftops all thatched or corrugated tin, the tall cylindrical graineries and outlying animal compounds made of rough brick the same color as the ground.

Mamadou—the largest village in the southern part of the valley, population somewhere around two thousand—although more and more strangers were arriving every week, farmers and herders from the countryside, fleeing the drought.

Things were getting to be so bad, Molly felt more than a little guilty to be leaving.

But tomorrow, well . . . it was all over with, wasn't it? No more clinic, no more Mamadou, no more Africa.

It was back to the real world for her. Back to the good old U.S. of A.

Damn.

Closing her eyes and taking a deep breath, Molly tipped her head back and let the sun wash over her face.

Who would've ever thought that this village would come to mean so much to her. And the clinic—a success beyond her wildest expectations. She remembered that day five months ago, way back in March, the morning she arrived from the capital and—

When the hand grabbed her arm, Molly nearly leapt out of her skin.

Pulling herself free, she spun around and had a second shock when she saw who was standing there, a leering grin twisting his emaciated face, his yellow bloodshot eyes gone wide.

Sibatia, the village lunatic, his hand reaching out for her once again, his fingers jabbing at the air as he stepped forward.

"Hey!" Molly said to him. "What the . . . ?"

He poked her once in the belly, hard, and then again, harder still.

A long peg tooth protruded from the side of his mouth as he quietly chuckled. He wore a stained white T-shirt, ripped ragged and filthy, and his black pants were hanging in shreds. His cracked rubber thongs were tied with loops of string around his ankles, and his legs and arms were covered with sores. Several large flies circled his knotted hair, buzzing loudly.

Smiling, he screwed up his face and sniffed the air, cocking his head to one side.

"It smells . . ." he said, staring intently into Molly's eyes. "It smells of . . . dirty cunt."

Startled, Molly backed away a few steps—and nearly fell headlong over the dog sitting in the path— Sibatia's mangy black mutt, which had somehow snuck up behind her. Head held low, it growled at her softly, foamy lips parting to reveal its jagged teeth.

"It smells of . . . America," Sibatia added, smiling and sniffing once again.

And then he began to sing, his voice gentle and light, the words in some strange language that Molly didn't recognize, but the tone unmistakable, lilting and sweet—the same haunting lullaby that her mother had sung in her dream.

Dazed and frightened, Molly stood there listening, as if hypnotized by the song.

14

Little by little the world around her seemed to fade . . . until nothing but Sibatia's voice remained, softly echoing through the emptiness, like sunlight rippling over the face of a deep, deep pool.

Never in her life had she heard anything so beautiful. Or so sad.

And then like a door slamming shut, Sibatia suddenly fell silent. Bowing to Molly, he abruptly turned and walked away, his feet kicking up puffs of red dust as he shuffled off, leaving the path to cut across an empty field.

That didn't really happen, Molly told herself. Did it?

How could he possibly know that song?

Her heart still fluttering in her chest, she watched him go, his thin, fleshless arms swinging at his sides, his legs badly bent as if from rickets. Trotting along behind him, the dog paused and turned back to gaze at her, its mouth cracking open in a prolonged yawn.

Jesus, Molly thought, her mind spinning in place. What the hell was that all about?

As far as she knew, most people in the village considered Sibatia to be harmless, nothing more than a poor crazyman, his mind touched by permanent fever.

But there were others who tended to shy away from even talking about him—people who, when pressed, would come out with the most incredible stories. Molly had even heard once that his mother had carried him in her womb for nearly two years.

For the most part, he seemed to spend his days and nights roaming aimlessly around the bush, although recently he'd begun trailing after Meru, the village shaman, following him everywhere like a faithful shadow. Maybe he'd grown attached to the old man, Molly thought, and Meru's unexpected death the other night had hit him especially hard. With the funeral and everything else going on today, well . . . the poor guy was probably upset.

Shading her eyes with her hand, Molly watched him crossing the dusty field, heading for the sacred grove.

A dense circle of mango trees and overgrown hedges, the grove sat in the center of a dry tobacco field, about two hundred yards from the outskirts of the village. The hedges were broken at only one point, a narrow passageway through which select men of the village could enter—elders and various bigshots, and young boys due to take part in certain secret rituals.

Objects of power were stored within the grove, treasures of the village and its people. Masks, holy talismans, ceremonial costumes and instruments, even a golden ingot. Meru, the keeper of the sacred grove, had always claimed that Mamadou's was the oldest grove in the entire country, the original from which all others had sprung.

As Molly watched, Sibatia reached the trees and slowly circled to his right. When he came to the opening in the hedge, he squatted on his heels in the shade, his black dog resting close beside him. Only then did Molly finally turn away, continuing on toward the village, that song replaying over and over in her mind, despite her every effort to forget it.

Later, when she entered her hut, she immediately found the gift that someone had left for her on her bed—a large green lizard wearing a tiny red apron, with a neat bloody hole gouged out between its splayed rear legs.

16

2

He waited until she was gone before he entered the grove, Pudzo running on ahead, tail wagging playfully.

He felt like a horny schoolboy, the way she always hardened him

When he closed his eyes, she was right there, watching from her seat by the door as he sang and worked on the little girl with his pliers and knife, as he lay beneath her on the floor and held her helplessly open, whispering sweet nothings into her little-girl ear.

When he closed his eyes, he saw her standing on the front steps of her precious clinic, the dead baby in her arms, a look of shocked disgust frozen on her face.

"It smells . . ." He laughed to himself, shaking his head and rousing the many flies settled on his hair. "It smells of America."

The grove was deserted, he was happy to see, with the exception of one old clown standing in front of Meru's hut, swinging his cane wildly at Pudzo.

"Why if it isn't Isaak, the *mganga*'s trusty assistant," Sibatia said, cutting through the herb garden that bordered the hut's front yard. "Surprise, surprise."

"Call off your dog," Isaak snarled, sweeping his cane back and forth through the air. "Damn you to hell, Sibatia. Call him off!"

Dancing nimbly from side to side, Pudzo stayed just

out of range, feinting and growling and showing his teeth, pawing at the ground like an angry bull.

"I think he likes you, Isaak," Sibatia said. "Get down on all fours, why don't you, and lift your robe. He'll show you a good time, I'm sure."

Taking an especially vicious swing, Isaak managed to connect, the knobby end of the cane smacking down solidly against the top of Pudzo's head. Wagging his tail harder than ever, Pudzo rolled over and played dead, then quickly leapt to his feet again, yapping happily.

"Take your demon hound and leave this place," Isaak spat out, stepping shakily backward, retreating toward the doorway of Meru's hut. "You have no business here."

"Oh, no?" Sibatia replied. Unzipping his pants, he pulled out his root and sent a stream of urine splashing into the flower bed alongside the path. "Actually, old man, I do."

When Pudzo trotted over, Sibatia aimed a ropy arc of piss into the dog's open mouth, Pudzo swallowing greedily, managing to capture every last golden drop.

"I warn you," Isaak said, lifting his cane high, ready to strike. "Leave here, or else."

"Be still," Sibatia said, zipping up.

Walking calmly over toward the old fellow, he reached out and placed his fingertips against Isaak's chest.

"Be still," he commanded again. "Behold a man touched by grace."

"How dare—" Isaak began, but then he abruptly fell silent, an almost comical expression of bug-eyed astonishment transfixing his face. His upraised arms trembled for an instant and then locked in place. His heart continued to beat along bravely for a little while longer, before finally tripping to a halt.

"That's better," Sibatia murmured as the old man crumpled to the ground in a heap. "Say hello to Jesus for me, Isaak."

Gripping him by the armpits, Sibatia dragged him inside the hut, Pudzo bouncing around now like a puppy.

"Hungry, boy?" Sibatia asked.

Lifting the corpse, he dumped it onto Meru's bed. Poor Isaak, the grief-stricken assistant, succumbing to a broken heart at the untimely death of his beloved master.

"Easy," Sibatia said as Pudzo leapt onto the bed and went for Isaak's throat. "You'll get some later, just relax."

Beginning with the shelf above the headboard, Sibatia worked his way around the room, searching through Meru's possessions. As he suspected he would, he found little of value—half a carton of German cigarettes, a pack of rubbers (assorted colors, deep-ribbed, extra-large), a pair of gloves made of crocodile skin, a magazine called *Yellow Women*—all of which he slipped into the cloth bag tied to his belt.

As for the rest—the prayer charts, the jars of medicines and salves, powders and colored vapors, the ceremonial shawls and gris-gris charms, the spirit beads and singing crystals, the bone rattles, jaguar tails, and wishing dolls, the vials of silver-blue dick dust and star pollen, the feather and shell fetishes, the chrisms, the black lizard skulls whispering to him from the shelf above the door—it was all just so much junk to him, costume props for a third-rate village magician, the sort of mumbo-jumbo crap he'd stopped playing with long before his nuts grew hair.

Oh well, he hadn't really been expecting much in the way of goodies, anyway. Not from Grandma Meru.

Leaving the charmist's hut with Pudzo at his heels, Sibatia walked off a ways into the trees, until he located a comfortable stump. Sitting down, he rummaged through his cloth bag for a moment, finally removing a small battered tin.

"Hey, boy," he said, snapping the container's lid open. "Let's get mystic. Let's get right."

Taking out three squares of black manilla paste, he closed the tin and slipped it back into the bag. Breaking off a corner of one cake, he gave it to Pudzo, then ate the rest himself. Chewing each bite thoroughly, he finished the first cake and then the others, fuel enough to carry him into orbit, or damn near.

Waiting for liftoff, he thumbed through *Yellow Women,* admiring the grace and beauty displayed on every page.

As the drug started to take effect, every little lady began to resemble the American girl, every grimacing inviting face, every pink pouting hole. The everpresent flies grew drowsy around his head, the paste coming alive within him, rising through his thoughts. Panting quietly, Pudzo began trotting in a tight circle, around and around, chasing his fleeing soul.

There was power in this grove—oh yes. He could feel it stirring right beneath him, locked deep within the ground. Waiting.

Slipping the magazine into his pouch and getting to his feet, Sibatia looked around for a suitable tree, spotting a fine old black gum just off to the left, its branches spread against the sky, the main bole straight and strong. Leaving Pudzo to his game, he walked over to it, windmilling his arms slowly, loosening the muscles and mixing up the blood. Getting a firm grip on the trunk, he started to climb, taking his time at first, measuring the character of the tree.

Five meters, ten—the ground steadily fell away as he ascended through the lower tiers of limbs. In his mother's womb, in his grave, and high in a sacred tree—nowhere else in this troubled world was a man truly at home.

Fifteen meters, twenty, and then suddenly he was above the canopy of the grove, with the village and fields spread out before him.

He could see people busy in the plaza, stacking wood in a large heap for tonight's funeral bonfire. He could see the soccer game going on in the dusty playing field behind the school bungalows, and the village elders gathered together in the shade of the giant acacia near the southern well, drinking beer and bullshitting about the good old days.

He was just reaching into his bag for a smoke when he happened to glance up and catch a glimpse of Reverend Red Flowers, his scarlet robe flashing through the branches, high overhead.

"Hey!" Sibatia hollered. "Hey, wait!"

Not wasting a moment, he started off after him, pulling himself heavenward. It had been a while since he'd last had a talk with the Reverend. Leaning away from the trunk, he peered into the upper reaches of the tree, and once again caught sight of the bloodred robe.

"Hey, monkey-nuts!" he yelled. "Hold on, will you?"

He climbed and climbed, the village dropping away below him, until soon he had a clear view of the entire valley, the river and the lunarlike terrain beyond. The higher he went, the brighter the sun became, filigrees of yellow and orange flaring and then fading across the sky, sky as blue as a Grandfather's eyes, each shifting design sounding a single sweet note of music as it disappeared, a constant stream of salutations to the gods.

Gradually, the tree itself began to change, the bark becoming as soft as velvet, the leaves all sparkling like the purest green crystal. Two unbroken columns of white ants made their way along the trunk—each ant marching upward carrying a small golden needle, while those heading down each held a tiny silver hoop. Pale lizards as fat as melons sat upon the largest limbs, whispering quietly to Sibatia as he climbed on by. Strange birds circled and cried, their glittering eyes regarding him coldly, black wings slicing through the hot still air.

Of the Reverend, there was no longer any sign. Giving up the chase, Sibatia sat for a moment and rested, fishing into his bag for another manilla wafer.

Looking down, he felt closer to the sky than the earth. The river was nothing more now than a thread unraveling from the mountains to the west, mountains like so many ripples on a puddle, the horizon beyond curving down and away. Here and there forests were burning, and armies swarmed like dark clouds across the vast, desolate plains.

Finishing his snack, Sibatia opened a pack of cigarettes and lit up. Perched above him, a lizard hissed seductively.

"Quite the songbird, isn't he?" it whispered. "I think the little booger's hungry."

"Fuck off, old man," Sibatia told it, recognizing the dead shaman's voice.

Peeling away a scrap of bark, he flicked it at the lizard and it scampered from sight. Standing, he adjusted his bag and resumed climbing.

As expected, the tree soon underwent further transformations.

The branches became bone, braided with sinews and tendons, and the jewel-like leaves vanished, replaced by tattered bits of skin. Fruits like organs hung from the limbs, purple-pink clumps of smooth flesh, fatty coral fans, and hearts faintly pulsing. Beads of bloody sap oozed from the trunk, and a thick odor of putrefaction fouled the air.

Sibatia climbed on, higher and higher. This was a fine, fine tree. A tree to remember.

Eventually, as he knew he would, he found the skull wedged in a fork, a bony nest padded with handfuls of long blond hair and snips of colored wire, the six black seeds lying snug within.

With the utmost care, while reciting the prescribed litany, he removed them one by one, gently swallowing each in turn, the moist gelatinous orbs shivering against his tongue as he forced them down. The last one gone, he closed his eyes and prayed.

"Is she the one?" a voice asked from above.

Looking up, Sibatia saw the Reverend sitting on a branch just overhead. Tall and spindly, his scarlet robe as luminous as his shiny skin, he smiled and raised a stick-thin arm, pointing behind Sibatia, his beetle-bright eyes sparkling.

"Is she?" he repeated.

Turning, Sibatia saw the city in the distance, spread out in all its splendor, the vast factories and cathedrals, the great boulevards as wide as rivers, the slaughterhouses belching multicolored smoke into the dusky brown sky. He saw the herds of white people roaming the avenues, racks of drying meat on every corner, the American airplanes passing silently over the stadiums and domed palaces, the soaring banks built of black glass and stone. He saw the gunboats patrolling the canals, and the caravans camped in the shadows of the temple ramparts. And high above the pinnacles of the obelisks and monuments, above the golden minarets and spires, the trestles, aqueducts, and silver-spun bridges arching over the city's streets and parks—in the tallest tower of them all, standing at a window on the uppermost floor, Sibatia saw the American girl, Molly—naked, her belly swollen and ripe, her eyes fixed on his—and *Yes,* he thought, *Yes, she's the one* . . .

Yes.

"Cute little ass," the Reverend noted, clicking his tongue as he idly stroked himself beneath his robe. "She your ticket to the Helly Deeps?"

"That's her," Sibatia replied.

His American Angel. His True Western Bride.

The proud bearer of his seed.

3

"Have you ever seen lions do it?" Rolfe asked Anne, sipping at his beer and staring into space. "Sometimes they keep at it for hours."

Please, Molly thought. Not that routine again.

She waited a moment, then pushed herself off the sofa. Crossing the room to the back door, she left Anne on her own with Rolfe.

Outside, under the stars, she dipped her cup into the pot of corn beer on the table. Dark and sweet, Mamadou homebrew was something she was certainly going to miss. There were stars in her cup when she brought it to her lips, stars sliding down her throat and rising behind her eyes.

God, what a day.

Up at dawn to finish packing, then spending all morning at the clinic doing paperwork—taking a break to attend Meru's funeral and the feast afterward—then back to the clinic again for the going-away party with the counselors. All those goodbyes and last minute details. And now this little get-together here, supper and beer and more goodbyes, Rolfe and Anne the last ones left, Rolfe with Anne; and me, Molly thought, me with my Mamadou beer. Just trying to forget about tomorrow and the three-hour drive with Rolfe to the capital, the flight to Cairo, the flight to Paris, to New York and finally Boston . . .

Off to the west along the horizon, flecks of lightning

shimmered in the sky, ghost lightning, bringing heat, not rain. Behind the walls surrounding her yard, the village was gearing up for the evening's activities. Soon the drumming would begin, the people gathering in the central plaza for the funeral dance in Meru's honor.

Molly took one of the leftover pancakes piled on the plate beside the pot of beer, dipping the end of it into the bowl of honey. As she ate she fingered the necklace of turquoise beads the women at the clinic had given her that morning.

For five long months they'd worked together—well, most of them had—and okay, sure, there'd been an occasional week off in the middle there, but damn if they hadn't gotten a lot accomplished. Designed and managed by Molly, and financed by World Vision, the Mamadou Mothers and Infants Center was up and running. The only clinic of its kind in the entire valley, it provided free counseling and a variety of services relating to child care and maternal health to anyone who needed it. And best of all, it was going to continue to do so, long after her departure tomorrow. Thanks to a dedicated staff, thoroughly trained by yours truly.

To a job well done, Molly toasted herself, lifting her cup high. *I knew you had it in you.*

"Hey," Anne said, coming through the back door. "Save some of that for me." Going over to the table, she found a cup and filled it.

They drank in silence for a moment, looking up at the star-heavy sky.

"So," Anne said at last. "You all set for tomorrow?"

"As set as I'm going to be."

"What time are you taking off, anyway?"

"Rolfe figures around six," Molly answered. "Don't remind me."

"I've decided I'm leaving on the fifteenth," Anne said. "That way I can stop in London to see some people I know, before heading on to the Big Apple."

For the past year or so, Anne and Rolfe had been working for Catholic Charities, teaching English and African history to villagers up and down the valley. Their funding had recently been cut, though, and Anne was making the trip back to the States to convince the bishops or whoever to fork over some more money.

"You looking forward to going home?" she asked.

Molly shrugged and sipped at her beer.

There was no denying that she missed Vermont. She'd been away since last summer, and it was going to be great to get back. And of course there was nursing school waiting for her, which was something she'd wanted to do for years now.

But still . . .

If World Vision had offered her another position, anywhere in Africa, she would've taken it in a minute.

"Not particularly, I guess," she finally answered.

"Yeah," Anne agreed. "I know what you mean."

A moment later, deep and sonorous, the first drums came alive in the plaza, calling everyone to the dance. Dogs barked and voices shouted, and a pack of kids went racing by beyond the fence, hooting and laughing.

"Hear that?" Rolfe asked, poking his head out the back door. "You guys ready yet, or what?"

"Yeah, yeah . . . we're coming," Anne told him, downing the last of her beer and setting the cup on the table. "Looks like it's time to go do some dancing."

Finishing her own beer, Molly followed Anne inside. Grabbing her camera off the shelf above the bed, she extinguished the two lanterns in the room.

"Sounds like the natives are getting restless." Rolfe laughed as they left the hut. "Man, what a beautiful night."

It sure was. Warm and still, with all those stars drifting overhead—the Grandmother, the Sow, the Jackal, and the rest looking down—a side of Heaven that Molly knew she might never see again.

The village was definitely much livelier than usual for this time of night, dogs and kids running every which way, rowdy teenagers with their radios turned too loud, elderly women with cloths draped over their heads, stepping aside and smiling politely as Molly, Rolfe, and Anne walked by.

Passing Mr. Bayma's store, they found a group of old men sitting on the porch, a kerosene lamp hissing on the steps beside them as they shared a few pots of beer. A small adobe house with a new zinc roof, in addition to batteries, spare bicycle parts, and cans of tomato paste from Zaire, Mr. Bayma's offered one of the finest front porches in the village, a popular spot to sit and lift a few, both night and day.

"What's happening?" Rolfe asked the men in French. *"Labass."*

"Labass," one of them replied, his yellow eyes glowering over his cup. *"Labass,* my ass."

Ominous and haunting, the low rumble of the drums echoed above the village, growing steadily louder as they neared the plaza. Bells and gourd rattles, tambourines and flutes, the music seemed to suddenly erupt as they rounded the last corner, almost

28

as if the villagers had been waiting for their arrival to actually begin the dance.

The plaza was packed with people, all on their feet and milling around, a huge bonfire rising in the center of the crowd, tall flames pulsing to the rhythm of the insistent drums.

Wanting to take some pictures while the fire was so high, Molly climbed onto a small pile of cordwood stacked before one of the huts along the perimeter of the plaza. Off to the right a group of dancing women had formed a large circle, their feet keeping up with every beat of the music, hands clapping and waving in the air. Near the fire, dressed in their long white robes, the musicians effortlessly maintained the rhythm, curved sticks pounding the cylindrical drums hanging at their sides, the bells, rattles, and tambourines driving right along with them, the flutes supplying a snappy little staccato melody, bright notes flashing like sparks above the crowd.

Molly took a couple shots of the bonfire, hoping it would come out looking half as creepy as it did through the lens.

Best seat in the house, she thought, watching all the action spread out around her. It seemed like just about everyone was dancing and swaying, old and young alike, the band really cooking now, wasting no time at all, the drummers taking turns trying to outdo one another, whooping and howling and egging each other on.

When these people bury someone, Molly thought, they certainly do it in style. First the funeral that morning, then the feast at noon, and now this little shindig here, which was likely to go on for hours.

Of course, Meru hadn't been just anyone. The village *mganga* for the past thirty-odd years, he had been one of the most respected men in the entire valley. Molly had spoken with him several times—a tough old guy, his skin wizened as a mummy's —a seer and diviner who was friendly with everybody, including bush spirits and djinns.

People went to him to have events such as sickness and death explained, or if they needed to get in touch with a loved one who'd died. Supposedly, back in his younger days, he'd given off so much light you could read by it.

Forever wrapped in a heavy hooded cape made of monkey skins, he'd always worn dozens of leather pouches looped around his neck, packed fat with mysterious amulets and ritual fetishes. No one had ever seen him eat anything but stones. He'd pluck up a rock and chew and chew, then spit out a mouthful of pebbles. Molly had watched him perform the trick more than once herself, and she still had no idea how he did it.

She was just about to climb down off the woodpile when the masks came charging out of the alleyway to her left, scaring the hell out of her and everyone else standing nearby.

Dressed in baggy costumes decorated with feathers, beads, and painted geometric designs, the half-dozen bearers rushed pell-mell into the crowd, swinging their oversized heads from side to side. Cackling with unearthly laughter, their fierce crocodile faces gleamed in the firelight as they chased the children away and made the women scream. Strange, otherworldly beings with tall headdresses made of hide and bone, their bellies swollen as if grotesquely pregnant, they dipped and twirled and shook, dancing their way toward the bonfire, the villagers parting to let them pass.

Camera in hand, Molly jumped down from the woodpile and started off after them, but she hadn't taken more than two steps before someone slid in front of her, blocking the way.

"Dorbi malo," he said. Stop, please.

Startled, Molly stepped back, failing at first to recognize the man in the bonfire's wild light.

"Tembro?" she asked.

"Yes, yes," he answered, nodding repeatedly, looking over both her shoulders and above her head, then down at his own nervously shuffling feet, anywhere but directly into her eyes. *"Malo, silga,"* he said. Please come.

The eldest son of Molly's landlord, for the past four months Tembro had been working as the clinic's part-time janitor.

"Malo!" he insisted, before Molly had a chance to speak. *"Wenafo ladde!"* Please! Something is wrong!

"Tembro, what is it?" Molly asked at last, thinking, Oh my God, the clinic's burning down. Or somebody's trashed it.

"Tim tonga," he told her, in a voice so halting he almost sounded in pain. Big trouble.

And then he abruptly turned and started walking away, leaving Molly standing there. Her heart racing in her throat, she glanced around at the dancing crowd, hoping that by some chance she might spot Rolfe or Anne.

"Milga, milga," Tembro called, turning back and waving impatiently, urging her on. Hurry.

31

"Shit," Molly muttered to herself, finally setting out after him.

All the time she'd known Tembro, she'd never once seen him upset. Whatever he'd found at the clinic must be pretty serious, for him to be in such a state.

"Wait," she called out. *"Kinkira,* Tembro."

But he had already rushed around the nearest corner.

Damn!

Scanning the sky above the rooftops for smoke, Molly hurried down one street and then another, Tembro trotting ahead of her, lighting his way with a flashlight. They passed a noisy clump of people, late arrivals heading for the plaza, the drums' thunder fading as they left the center of the village behind.

Halfway to the clinic she caught up with him at last, and less than a minute later they were there. Molly let out a deep sigh of relief when she found the hut still standing, the lights out and the front door closed, everything apparently in one piece.

But when she turned toward Tembro, he looked even more agitated than before.

"Bondo? Bondo don far?" he said, his voice toneless as he pointed his flashlight at the stoop, the thin beam wavering in his shaking hand: There? See it?

Yes, she did. A small round bundle lying on the top step.

A pillow? A sack of rice?

For one crazy moment she thought it might be a baby. And then, as she stepped closer, she realized that was exactly what it was.

A baby, wrapped in a yellow and black shawl . . . a sleeping baby, its tiny face lit by Tembro's light.

Unbelievable.

Someone had actually left their kid lying on the front steps of the clinic.

Bending down, Molly carefully scooped it up in her arms—and instantly saw that it was dead. Its eyes were partially open and clotted with grit, and a thick dusting of sand coated its skin.

But that wasn't all.

A tortured groan escaped her throat. God help her, she knew this baby.

Four days ago a nomad family had come to the clinic with a sick infant—severely malnourished, dehydrated, burning with fever—ill beyond helping. It had died that night, and they'd buried it the next morning, wrapped in a black and yellow shawl.

"Oh, no," Molly moaned, her voice full of dread.

Who could have done this? Who could have dug up a baby's corpse?

And then Tembro began to hum the song, soft and lilting, the same song Molly's mother had sung in her dream.

Molly spun around so quickly, she nearly toppled off the stairs.

Tembro looked up at her in some sort of trance, his eyes rolling back until only the whites were showing, his mouth hanging open and his tongue quivering against his teeth. From deep in his chest the lullaby rose, gentle and sweet.

"Quite the songbird, isn't he?" a voice said.

A black dog came slinking out of the shadows, and then Sibatia stepped around the corner of the hut, his pocked face lit by a broad grin.

For a long moment no one moved, not even the dog.

33

Tembro paused, and then fell silent. The only sound was the muffled drums coming from the plaza, drifting over the darkened village.

Finally, Sibatia broke the spell.

Chuckling softly, he stepped forward and reached up, touching the baby's brow with his fingertips. Instantly, the infant's eyes snapped open.

Squirming restlessly, it stared up at Molly, its tiny jaws working as it stretched out a dusty hand toward her, fingers clutching weakly at the empty air.

"I think the little booger's hungry," Sibatia said.

"Jesus!" Molly shouted.

In one panicky motion she bent down, dropped the baby, and leapt off the steps onto the grass. She landed awkwardly, the dog growling and scrambling toward her, as Sibatia clapped his hands and laughed.

Before she could recover her balance, Tembro came after her, rearing back and kicking her full-force in the belly, knocking her to the ground.

Still laughing, Sibatia walked up and put his hands on her forehead, and suddenly everything was gone. . .

She was back in that room again, naked, lying on the floor. Someone was beneath her, holding her tight and whispering in her ear.

Sitting on the benches against the walls, there were at least a dozen Sibatias, all watching her closely.

Yes, the man under her said. *Yes, she's the one.*

And then each of the Sibatias slowly stood and came toward her, each carrying a knife and a rusty pair of pliers.

Oh, yes . . .

4

When her eyes jerked open, Molly found herself sitting at a small wooden table. Tembro was in a chair across from her, staring down at the dead baby in his arms, its face pressed against his bare chest.

When she tried to push herself away from the table, she discovered that she couldn't move. Her hands were right out in front of her, resting on top of the table, but it was as if they belonged to somebody else. No matter how hard she tried to move them, they just stayed lying there. And she couldn't do anything with her legs either. In fact she couldn't feel a thing below her waist. She could turn her head slightly from side to side, but only with great difficulty, and even then it was merely a matter of inches.

Her skull was humming with fear. When she attempted to speak, the most she could manage was a weak moan in the back of her throat, a sheeplike bleat of terror.

"Shhh . . . *tillis*." Tembro hissed, tipping his chin toward the baby in his lap. Quiet.

He glanced up at her for a moment, his face expressionless, mouth agape, his eyes still showing nothing but white.

Molly groaned again. Overcome by panic, she strained with all her might, willing herself to move. Her right thumb twitched once, twice, and then lay still.

A tear ran down her cheek, her blood booming in

her ears. Her body was like a dead thing, no longer under her control.

Desperate, she looked around the room. Two windows, both with the curtains pulled tightly shut, an unmade bed in one corner, a small dresser, a wooden stool, and a couple of empty shelves.

Tembro's hut? Is that where I am?

On the table sat a half carton of German cigarettes, a magazine called *Yellow Women,* and her own camera. According to the watch on her wrist, it was almost one in the morning. She'd lost four hours.

Outside the hut, everything was quiet.

She tried to speak again, and this time woke the baby. It pulled away from Tembro's breast, and Molly saw the open wound where Tembro's nipple should've been, a puffy gash, the blood smeared across the baby's face.

Creaking noisily, a door suddenly swung open behind her.

The black dog came into sight first, circling under the table to nuzzle its snout roughly into Molly's crotch. Then the door slammed shut and Sibatia was standing there, dressed in a Grateful Dead T-shirt, bright Bermuda shorts, and a pair of strange scaly gloves, his long greasy hair slicked back close to his skull.

"Hey, kids," he said, licking his lips in a lizardly way. "Sorry to keep you waiting."

Gurgling happily, the dead baby waved its hands in the air. Craning his neck around, Tembro muttered and stared off into the distance, his blunt yellow teeth chattering together as he idly fingered the hole in his chest.

"Easy there, Pudzo," Sibatia said softly, calling off the dog.

He gave Molly an apologetic shrug, then reached into the burlap bag tied to his belt and took out a six-inch knife and a rusty pair of pliers, setting them both on the table beside Molly's outstretched arms.

"He's just impatient," he explained, leaning down until his face was only an inch or so from hers. "But who can blame him?"

For a second Molly thought he was about to kiss her. Lips twitching, he sighed and rested a hand on the back of her neck. His breath was cold and had an odd metallic odor to it. Scores of pale blue flies rode in his hair, all of them silent, as if waiting.

"Such a lovely," he told her, bringing his other hand up to gently cup her left breast. "Such a prize."

A long interminable moment passed as he caressed her through her blouse. His eyelids fluttered shut and he sighed deeply once again. Bowing his head for just an instant, he murmured something that Molly couldn't quite hear. Then he abruptly straightened and stepped away, the flies in his hair all erupting frantically into flight.

Plucking the camera off the table, he handed it to Tembro, taking the baby from his arms.

"For your scrapbook." He smiled at Molly, moving to stand beside the dog.

Tembro clicked off a total of four shots, Sibatia posing like a proud father, the dead infant cooing obligingly and making goofy faces. When the roll of film was finished, Tembro set the camera down and took back the baby, guiding it to the wound in his chest once again, its tiny fists eagerly kneading his flesh as it fed.

"Okay," Sibatia said, an almost regretful tone thickening his voice. "Okay, let's do it."

Walking around behind Molly, he grabbed her by the hair and yanked her head backward. Bending down, he locked his mouth to hers, clenching her face firmly with his other hand, forcing her jaws wide open.

He coughed once, and then again, his belly heaving as he vomited the first seed into her throat.

PART 2

~

The foul
realities

CHAPTER TWO

1

The moment Charlie Coughlin saw his daughter step off the seven o'clock bus from Boston, he knew something was wrong. Sure, he hadn't seen her in more than six months, but all it took was one glance for him to tell what sort of lousy shape she was in.

"Hey, Daddy!" she laughed, walking into his arms.

"Hi, honey." He gave her a long squeeze, kissing her forehead and tousling her hair. "Welcome home."

"Yeah." She stepped back and looked around the grimy bus-station parking lot, smiling brightly. "I can't believe I actually made it."

"Rough trip?"

"I'll say. Hold on a second."

Thanking the driver, she collected her suitcase from the belly of the bus. There was just one other passenger getting off in Brattleboro, so it only took a moment.

"Where's Mom?" she asked as Charlie took the bag from her.

41

"Fixing supper."

"Don't tell me. Lasagna?"

"Are you kidding? Two giant pans of the stuff. Enough to last a week."

"You wish. I'm eating it all tonight."

Charlie laughed along with her, but inside he was thinking: Man, does she look terrible. Her face was pale and there were dark circles around her eyes. Her shoulder-length hair was unbrushed and her jeans were dirty and torn at one knee. She was also skinnier than hell.

"Whoa, a new car!" she said as Charlie opened the rear door of the wagon and slid the suitcase inside. "I'm impressed."

"The old one finally died for good," he told her. "Rusted away on us to nothing. One day the gas tank fell off, right there in the driveway." He held the keys out toward her. "You want to drive home?"

"I don't think so, Daddy. I'm beat."

When he went to start it, the car sputtered and coughed, but he got it going on the second try. Pulling out onto Putney Road, he gave it a little extra gas.

"So," he asked, "it wasn't a good trip?"

Flying halfway around the world—it was hard for Charlie to even begin to imagine. One day you're in the middle of Africa, and the next you're back here in Vermont.

"Not too bad, I guess," Molly answered. "The bus from Boston was probably the worst part."

They were coming into town now, the movie theater on the right and the Grand Union just ahead. At the next intersection, they caught the red light and Charlie slowed to a stop.

"You don't look so hot," he told her. "You've lost a lot of weight, or something."

Molly shrugged. "A few pounds, maybe."

More like fifteen or twenty, Charlie thought. Easy.

He pulled the car onto Main Street, braking to let an old lady go by on the crosswalk. Molly looked around at the stores, the newly remodeled Bank of Vermont on the corner of Maple, the Friday-evening shoppers strolling up and down the sidewalk, the crowd of kids outside the video arcade.

"So how's Mom doing?" she asked.

"Fine, fine. Hanging in there."

No sense telling her the latest news now, Charlie figured. This wasn't the time or the place. Besides, Helen had decided she should be the one to let Molly know about the most recent round of tests.

Tomorrow, maybe . . .

Charlie turned onto Maple and followed it until they reached River Street, leaving town behind them. "It's sure great to have you back," he said, still thinking of Helen's troubles. "We missed you."

"Well, I missed you guys too," she replied. "Now that I'm here, it feels like I've been away forever."

There were a few more houses, then a stretch of nothing but trees, the road winding through a series of long looping curves.

"Damn," Charlie muttered, slowing the car.

"What's wrong?"

"The Grand Union. I was supposed to stop for some stuff." As soon as the road straightened out, he eased onto the shoulder, letting a couple of cars go by before he turned around. "Your mother will kill me if I don't go back."

43

Retracing their route—River to Maple to Main—five minutes and two red lights later they pulled into the store's mostly empty parking lot.

"Remember before you left?" Charlie said, turning off the ignition. "There was all that fuss about them wanting to build a Wal-Mart out on White Hill Road?"

"Yeah, I remember."

"Well, they went ahead and built it after all. First Wal-Mart in southern Vermont. It opened last week. You coming in with me?"

"No, I think I'll just wait here."

"You need anything? How about some ice cream?"

"God, ice cream. What's that?"

"I'll be right back," he told her, climbing out of the car. "Won't be more than a minute."

Entering the supermarket, taking a basket from the stack by the door, Charlie made his way down the fruit and vegetable aisle. Heading for the beer area, he grabbed two quarts of Bud, cold ones from the back of the shelf.

Parmesan cheese for the lasagna, a fresh loaf of bread from the bakery, a bottle of Russian salad dressing, and two half gallons of chocolate fudge swirl, Molly's favorite flavor ever since she was a kid.

Up front at the register, waiting for some old guy in the express lane to pay for a hundred cans of cat food, Charlie pulled a *Weekly World News* out of the rack.

Reincarnation shocker! Unborn baby speaks from Mom's womb! . . . New wave of angel sightings! Is the end of the world near? . . . Video voodoo! Witch doctors use videotapes to put curses on their enemies! . . . Alien insects found at Florida resort!

44

Turning to the horoscope page, Charlie checked out this week's forecast.

Get ready for action! Take a few risks!

Branch out in a new direction and just watch things grow! Your ideas are going to bear real fruit at last!

Dream all you want! Don't let anyone tell you it's a waste of time!

A loved one does something that really surprises you in a way you hadn't anticipated. It's because they care!

Not bad, he decided, returning the paper to its slot. Not bad at all.

ANGUISH OVER AFRICA, said the copies of *Time* in the next rack. CAN AFRICANS OVERCOME THEIR HISTORY?

The cover showed the obligatory naked, starving kid, complete with twig arms, huge Keanelike eyes, and a swollen belly.

"Hey, Charlie," Adell said at the register, giving him a cockeyed grin. "How's it going?"

Charlie set the magazine on the conveyor. "Hi, Adell."

"Your daughter get home yet?" Without wasting a single movement, she waved everything past the scanner. "That's seventeen fifty-three. I saw Helen in here the other day and she told me the good news. Paper or plastic?"

"Paper, please," Charlie said, fishing out his wallet. "As a matter of fact, I just picked Molly up at the bus station."

While Charlie counted the bills onto the conveyor,

Adell stacked all the groceries neatly into a paper bag, saving the bread for last.

"Well, you tell her I said hello, okay?"

"You bet."

"I've told Helen I don't know how many times, I hope you're both proud of that girl. There's not a lot of people around that could do what she does."

"No fooling," Charlie said, handing her eighteen dollars. "I sure couldn't."

"Me neither. Not in a million years."

"See you later, Adell," Charlie said, pocketing his change and grabbing the bag. "Say hi to that no-good husband of yours."

"See you, Charlie. You take care now."

Goddamn, he thought, as soon as he stepped outside. He'd forgotten to buy some prune juice.

He was debating whether or not to go back for it when he noticed that the front seat of the Toyota was empty and the passenger door partially open.

Where'd she take off to?

Approaching the car from behind, Charlie saw Molly suddenly sit up. As he circled around to the driver's side he spotted the small wet patch on the pavement outside her door, a glistening gob of . . . what? Vomit?

"You okay?" he asked, climbing in and setting the groceries on the seat between them.

"Yeah," she told him, keeping her head turned away for a moment as she closed the door and wiped her mouth. "I think I ate something on the plane that didn't agree with me, that's all."

"You sure?"

"Daddy, don't worry, I feel fine. Really." She

46

leaned over and peered into the bag. "Believe me, it's nothing a little ice cream and lasagna won't cure."

Looking at her, Charlie had his doubts, but he decided to keep them to himself. As he started the car, Molly pulled the *Time* from the bag and began flipping through it.

"I thought you might want to see that," he said, backing out of his slot, then driving across the parking lot. "Seems like every day something else is going on over there."

"You think it's bad now, just wait another few years." Molly stared ahead through the window, her hands still turning the pages of the magazine. "Africa's like a sick pig wallowing in its own shit, waiting to be slaughtered. Revolution, civil wars, famine, drought, disease, refugees . . ." Her voice trailed off.

Charlie didn't know what to say. Sometimes, it scared him thinking about the things she'd seen over there.

They drove in silence for a while, leaving town for a second time.

"Don't tell Mom I'm not feeling so hot, okay?" Molly said, giving him a weary smile. "She'll just start worrying."

"You sure it's only something you ate?" Charlie asked.

"Yeah," she told him. "I'm sure."

And then they were home, Charlie pulling into the driveway, giving the horn a couple fancy beeps as he parked behind the Winnebago.

Helen and Harley came hurrying out the front door together, Helen all smiles and Harley barking away.

By the time Helen and Molly were finished hugging, both of them were crying, and Charlie was close to tears himself.

"Home sweet home." Molly laughed, opening the back of the car and lifting out her suitcase.

Pausing to glance around the yard, Molly's gaze lingered for a moment on the towering old maples bordering the road. Finally, she turned and followed her parents inside.

Later, in the kitchen, Charlie opened a quart of Bud and filled three glasses.

"A toast," he announced, handing the beer around. "To the prodigal daughter's return."

They stood there grinning at one another, Charlie thinking to himself that this was one of those moments you hope you never forget. They clinked their glasses together and drank, then Charlie poured some of his beer into Harley's bowl next to the fridge, Harley's tail whapping against the wall as he lapped it down.

"Say, what's all this?" Molly said, looking around the kitchen.

"Your mother and I have been fixing the place up some," Charlie told her. "We put this new floor down ourselves, and replaced the old cabinets."

"Yes, and it only took us about three months." Helen laughed. "My knees still hurt me, from all the crawling we did on that linoleum."

"Good work can never be rushed, right?" said Charlie. "And everyone knows it takes knees forever to heal."

He set his beer down on the counter and went over to the refrigerator. He took out the bowl of lettuce he'd picked from the garden earlier, a cucumber, a carrot and some celery, a green pepper, a red onion, and a few ripe tomatoes. He lined everything up, found the knife, and got busy making the salad.

"Need some help, Dad?" Molly asked.

"No, you just relax."

Helen opened the oven and checked the lasagna, testing the noodles with a fork. "I better get the table set, this is nearly done."

"Mmmm, smells great." Molly leaned over the stove and inhaled. "It smells like . . . I don't know . . . like America."

"Hot dogs smell like America," Charlie told her. "Say, why don't you give your sister a call and tell her you're home?"

Molly raised her glass and sipped her beer. "Okay, why not?"

"That's her number right there on the board beside the phone," Helen said.

Molly dialed and waited, letting it ring. "I guess nobody's home," she finally said.

Finished with the lettuce and tomatoes, Charlie poured himself another half glass of beer.

"No thanks, Dad," Molly told him when he offered her a refill. "I think I'll help with the table. How's Linda doing, anyway?"

"No comment," Charlie said. "Ask your mother."

"She's just fine," answered Helen. "Arthur's out of work again, but—"

"So what else is new?" Charlie added.

"—but the kids are all doing great, and, well . . . they'll manage somehow. You know your sister."

Molly and Helen headed into the dining room, each carrying a stack of dishes and bowls. Doing his best to put all thoughts of Arthur out of his mind, Charlie chopped away at the vegetables, keeping the pieces uniformly small. When Molly returned to the kitchen, she stood at his side for a moment, snitching slices of green pepper from the bowl.

"Remember how when you and Linda were kids," he said, "you got an allowance every week? You set and cleared the supper table, fed the dog, kept your rooms clean and so on, for a dollar a week?"

"You never paid us a dollar, Daddy. It was always fifty cents."

"Whatever," Charlie said. "I always paid you something, for chores you kids probably should've been doing for free anyway. But I've been thinking. I don't know if you're planning on getting a job right away, before school starts, but there's plenty of things you could do around here, things I never seem to find the time to do myself."

"Such as?"

"Well, the place needs to be painted, for one thing. That'll take you a while, a few weeks at least, depending on whether or not you do the trim. And the flower gardens along the back of the yard could stand a major overhaul. The borders need to be redone, and all the beds built up. The weeds are pretty much out of control, and I know your mother wants to get some new plants in there."

"Plus the pool needs to be repaired, and the driveway resealed, and I guess the garage could use a better roof," Helen said, coming back into the kitchen. "Honestly, Charlie. She's been home less than an hour, and already you're putting her to work."

"Forget the pool for now, and the driveway can wait too," he said. "I was going to tackle it myself, next week, but if you want to do it, Molly, I'd be glad to show you how."

"Exactly what were you thinking of paying me?"

"Depends on the job, or we could do it by the hour, I suppose. You tell me."

"Whatever you decide, get it down in writing, honey." Helen shut off the oven and took out one of the pans of lasagna. "You can bring the bread, and I'll take this in. Charlie, that salad looks finished to me. Let's eat."

"Okay, I'll just cut the rest of this carrot."

He took a couple more whacks at it, then gave the knob to Harley. If there was another dog in the world who loved to eat raw carrots, Charlie had never met him.

Tomatoes, peppers, cucumbers—Helen was right, the salad was done.

Downing the remainder of his beer, Charlie set his glass in the sink, and grabbing the salad bowl, he turned and followed his wife and daughter into the other room.

Supper over and the dishes done, they took their coffee out onto the patio. The sun was down, but the western sky was still a wash of pale red and gray. While Molly and Helen admired the vegetable garden, Charlie smoked a cigarette and scratched Harley's head.

He was on his second cup of coffee before the tour was complete. Helen had baked a cheesecake that afternoon, one of her chocolate-strawberry specials. As she sliced them each a generous piece, Molly disappeared inside for a moment, then returned with two small packages.

51

"Here you go, folks," she said. "Exotic gifts from the heart of the dark continent."

Helen opened hers first—a pair of thin brownish-tan gloves that shimmered and sparkled in the waning light. Snakeskin? Charlie wondered. They looked about ten sizes too large, until Helen tried them on.

"Perfect fit." Molly laughed. "That's crocodile, by the way. They're ceremonial gloves, worn during rituals and blessings and stuff."

"They're beautiful," said Helen. "Really."

"Kind of sexy," Charlie noted. "Nice and soft too."

When he unwrapped his present, he found a pack of German cigarettes—Stuyvesants—and a small black skull, not much larger than a golf ball.

"It's a lizard," Molly informed them. "A tree lizard."

Charlie held it up and looked it in the eye. "Cute little bastard, isn't he?"

"It's supposed to be magic," Molly explained. "At certain special times, like when you need some advice, or maybe a warning or something, if you hold it up to your ear, and you're lucky, it'll talk to you."

Charlie gave it a try. He cocked his head and listened for a moment, concentrating.

"Okay, hold on," he said. "It's for you," he told Helen. "Long distance."

But she wouldn't touch it. "No thanks, it gives me the creeps. Just take a message."

Charlie laughed and dropped the skull carefully into his shirt pocket, then went ahead and had seconds on the cake. What the hell, he'd already had two helpings of lasagna. He listened to Helen and Molly discuss the doings of the neighbors, news of Molly's old friends and Helen's job, adding his own two cents now and then, but mostly just listening. The conversation had been going nonstop since supper, and personally, he was just about talked out.

At nine o'clock he got up and turned on the patio lights. "How about a swim?" he suggested.

"Actually, I think I better just go to bed," Molly replied. "I can hardly hold my eyes open."

When Charlie kissed her good night, and she said, "See you in the morning, Daddy," it sounded so good, he kissed her again.

Helen went along inside with her, and left alone on the patio, Charlie tried one of the German cigarettes. A bit strong maybe, but then he was used to smoking menthols.

After a while Helen came back outside. She cut herself another thick slice of cheesecake and gave half to Harley. A soft breeze rustled the dogwoods and Japanese maples on either side of the patio, and Charlie glanced up at the first stars gracing the night sky.

"She doesn't look very good, does she?" Helen said quietly. "And she hardly ate a thing at supper."

"If you ask me," Charlie told her, "she looks like she's been through a pretty rough time."

"Well, she probably has." Helen set her fork down and sighed. "But she's home now."

"Yeah, thank God, she's home." For just an instant Charlie remembered the Grand Union parking lot, but he quickly pushed the thought from his mind. "Safe and sound."

"Tomorrow after lunch, I think I'll take her shopping in town, or maybe over to Greenfield, to Sears."

"What for?"

"For whatever she wants. I know she needs a

53

bathing suit and some new jeans. You can come along with us, if you like."

Charlie shrugged. Shopping for clothes was Helen's department. "So, when are you going to tell her about the latest tests?"

"In the morning, I suppose. I just didn't want to ruin tonight."

Charlie reached over and held her hand for a moment as Harley chased a moth around the patio, snapping his teeth in the air. High overhead, a plane crossed the sky, gliding through the stars.

"I think I'll go in and give Linda another call," Helen said. "Just to let her know that Molly made it home okay."

"Tell her to come over tomorrow for supper. Bring the kids, but leave that deadbeat husband of hers at home. I'll cook some burgers and corn on the grill."

Collecting the dessert dishes, the coffee cups and plates, Helen piled everything on the tray. Charlie got up and held the door for her, Harley dashing inside at the last second, chewing away at something, most likely the moth.

While Helen used the phone, Charlie switched on the television to the movie they'd been advertising all week—the cop with the split personality, one half keeps killing teenage prostitutes, while the other half tries to track him down. Not exactly believable, but Charlie figured he'd give it a chance.

"Linda won't be able to make it tomorrow," Helen said, coming into the living room and sitting down on the sofa. "They've got car trouble again, but hopefully it'll be fixed by Sunday, so they'll be over then. What's this?"

On the screen, a pretty young girl was brushing her

hair in a motel bathroom, while the killer-cop waited in bed, playing with his knife.

"Nothing much," Charlie said, reaching for the remote. "I think we've already seen it."

Charlie ran through the channels, up one way and down the other, before settling on the Red Sox and Yankees at Fenway.

"Well, if you're watching baseball, I'm going to sleep," Helen told him. "Or maybe I'll read for a while."

"Wake me up early tomorrow morning, if I'm not already awake," Charlie said. He gave her rear end a pat as she leaned over the chair to kiss him. "And don't you worry about Molly. She's just exhausted from her trip. A couple days taking it easy, and she'll be good as new again. You'll see."

"I hope you're right. Anyway, I'm glad she's home."

"Me too. See you tomorrow."

"Good night, Charlie."

It turned out to be a poor excuse for a ball game. The Yankees were up six to one by the fifth inning, but Charlie stuck with it. The Sox had been winning some tough games this season, and anything might happen.

But when the Yankees added two more runs in the seventh, Charlie lost interest. He started thinking about the girls—Molly with that itch of hers to travel, to always be going somewhere else, and Linda with three kids already, no money, and a husband who couldn't keep a job. Any job.

One thing Charlie knew for certain, if Helen took another turn for the worse, they were going to have to really pull together for her. All they had was each other, and now that the cancer had returned, Helen would need them more than ever.

At the next Red Sox pitching change, Charlie decided to switch back to the movie. Halfway there, he stopped at PBS for what looked like a nature show on Africa.

Brown hills and trees, and a herd of wild things like deer. A lion stalking through the tall dry grass. The herd shifted nervously, peering into the distance. Then another lion crept forward and the herd broke and ran . . .

Charlie nodded off before the end of the show, and slept for nearly an hour. At one point, as his dreams turned sour, a small voice rose from his shirt pocket, singing a soft lullaby.

2

Naked, she stood before the full-length mirror, examining the wound between her legs.

Scabs like bloodied raisins flaked onto her hands. Pus seeped, but there was surprisingly little pain. Tugging at a few hardened clumps of hair, her fingers lingered for a moment, one nail lightly probing a crusty blister.

I'm a goddamn train wreck, she thought, eyeing her reflection. Gaunt, potbellied, pale as paper—what will Uncle Dry Skull say when he receives me?

Hello, little egg sac? Hello, my empty husk?

Inside her, they were starting up again, Molly thinking no way could she last through another night of this. By morning, with any luck, there would be pieces of her scattered in every corner of the room.

Bending over, she released a prolonged whistling

sigh of foul gas from her rectum, the by-product of her composting bowels.

"Hollow me out," she whispered, pressing her hands to her rounded womb. "Unravel my insides and splinter my spine."

Frisky and eager, she could feel the six of them in there, all quicksilver cozy, rooting gently through the sweetest scraps.

Turning away, she walked over to her desk, where two old candy tins sat waiting. Holding one against each breast, she carried them to her bed. Pushing aside several stuffed toys and a whole crowd of dolls, she stretched out on the mattress, leaning back against the headboard.

Opening the smaller tin, she removed a square black wafer, one corner of which she immediately bit off. The year's first golden honey, fresh summer cream, strawberries warm from the sun. The manilla cake dissolved in her mouth, each bite more delicious than the last.

From the second tin she took out the lizard, straightening its little red apron before she laid it on her stomach.

She could hear the television droning in the other room, but otherwise the world was quiet and still. Outside her window, crickets chirred beneath the rising moon. If she closed her eyes and concentrated, she could just make out the sound of drums, a dreamy pulsing from deep in the woods behind the house.

When the lizard stirred, she placed a comforting hand upon its back, smiling down at it as it blinked and yawned and stretched itself awake.

"Here you go," she said, offering it a small piece of wafer. "Hey, you hungry?"

The lizard sat up and took the cake from her with its tiny green hands, its tail brushing back and forth. As it chewed, the crumbs spilled from the gaping hole in its belly, sprinkling onto Molly's skin.

It wasn't much longer before she began to drift off. Groggily, she reached for the four photographs lying on the night table. Earlier, when she had shown her parents the pictures she'd brought home from Africa, Molly had set these few aside, the very last shots taken on her final night in Mamadou, mementos from the Other Side.

In the first photograph, Sibatia was beaming broadly, dressed in his Bermuda shorts and Grateful Dead T-shirt. Held in his arms, the dead baby was cooing happily, while the black dog sat at his feet. Staring directly at the camera, everyone's eyes were burning red jewels, demon eyes, demented and bright.

In the next photo, the three of them had obviously begun to rot. They were still smiling, but their flesh was peeling from their bones. Deep putrescent sores pitted their faces, arms, and legs. The baby's belly was bloated with corruption, and the dog was nearly hairless now, its swollen black tongue hanging from its mouth.

In the third picture, muscles and gray-green bones were fully exposed. The dog's internal organs were clearly visible, pink streamers of intestine like chains of sausage. The baby's soft skull had expanded obscenely, and Sibatia's face was a jellied mass, festooned with ragged strips of tissue and scalp.

In the last shot, a skeleton wearing colorful shorts and a tie-dyed T-shirt held a skeleton baby in his arms, a skeleton dog sitting at his feet.

Recalling the feel of those bones against her flesh,

an expansive calm settled over Molly. Returning the photographs to the night table, she let her mind wander off to play by itself. When the seeds began to rise inside her without warning, at first she struggled to keep them down, her throat spasming painfully as she swallowed repeatedly, sucking in air.

A true warrior has no time for retreats or regrets, she reminded herself. *A true warrior has nothing to fear.*

One after another the six dark eggs slid from her mouth, Molly carefully catching each one and placing it beside her on the mattress. Letting out a high, skirling whistle, the lizard leapt up and turned several cartwheels across the foot of the bed, then scampered over to the candy tin to help itself to another bite of cracker.

Lord, get my room ready, Molly thought, watching the seeds shivering on the sheet. My lonely days are finally done.

Clambering over each other like six starving piglets jostling for position around a single teat, all the seeds started frantically pressing themselves together. Molly heard a loud sizzling sound like meat frying on an open flame, and then suddenly there was only one large seed sitting on the bed, a quavering ebony melon, a jiggling ball of congealed nightmare.

When the crimson-lipped mouth irised open on its crown, Molly slowly leaned forward and peered inside.

Were those really stars in there?

CHAPTER THREE

⟋

Do it," she bleated. "Do it now."

So many worlds. So many that have passed, and so many more still to come.

In one world the Uncles may all creep on their bellies, in another they may live in the water like fish. Perhaps in a world to come, Uncles will fly and never leave the trees.

Or they might, in some wonderful world, do nothing but dream . . .

Gripping him just so, her muscular insides urged forth his sap.

"Ooh," she whined. "A sweet, sweet delight, no?"

She raised her rosy ass, her windy fundament, a mother of an ass, the odor of desire wafting through the air, a pungent fusty dew.

He plunged deeper into her, deeper into God's own law.

Holding him in a scissored caress, she spread her taut rear legs, her svelte haunches, exposing the plump rift between her thighs, the wound that never heals.

His manly parts nicely hardened, he slipped into her snuggest vent. Everything was splashy. Clutching her breasts, he felt her nipples like tiny tumors flexing with pleasure.

"Ooh, chummy," she purred.

Her soft sugared sounds soon turned to high-tone growls as she received his fluids, her bony skull knocking against the ground.

Looking west toward America all the while, toward Chicago and New York, Sibatia emptied both of his balls into the Auntie's dorsal reservoir. As the last driblets drained from his toasty loins, he shoved her aside, spraying his seed onto the ground, ivory-blue pearls sparkling in the sun.

Time to get planted.

While he caught his breath, the Auntie bowed to him in thanks and staggered away. Sitting up, Sibatia considered for a few moments, then removed a pocket calculator from a small rawhide pouch fastened to his belt. Punching some buttons, he examined the result, then replaced the calculator, closing the pouch securely.

Many and various, different in size and unlike in temperament, the Grandfathers traversed in all directions the depths of space.

How best to determine the percentage dead? Dead but still with us, they dreamt on yet, doomed to dilapidation in solitary splendor, guardians of the dark moon.

And what of the rogues, the Grandfathers who drift too close? Traveling incognito, they career along their orbits, prograde and retrograde. Subject to inflammation, they exhaust the juices of the Earth, bringing pestilence and famine, revelations and war.

Someday, they will come to us without restriction from all quarters, running like horses across the field of space . . .

A sudden gut-twisting shriek of pain erupted from the nearby brush, distracting Sibatia from his reverie. A moment later Pudzo appeared in the dry grass, a ragged strip of flesh clutched in his mouth.

Trotting over to Sibatia, he spat it out onto his master's lap, Sibatia wetting both of his forefingers and shoving them deep into the dog's ears.

"Good boy," he said, though of course Pudzo couldn't hear a thing. Extracting one finger, he reached down and affectionately fondled the dog's stones. "Good boy."

Breaking off a corner of the meat, he tossed it into the brush, Pudzo barking and chasing after it. Pausing for a minute to lick himself erect, the dog settled down to devour the scrap of Auntie.

Turning away, Sibatia attempted to refocus his thoughts on the Old Ones, but the afterglow of his session with the lissome bitch was rapidly fading. Yawning, more spent than inspired, he stood and stretched his limbs, folding the remaining flesh into the back pocket of his shorts.

Might as well go visit his ma, he decided. Although he much preferred the graveyard after dark, he had a busy evening ahead of him, so now was probably the best time to pay his respects.

Skirting the clump of shrubs where the moaning Aunt lay, Sibatia headed for the village. A dozen pale flies followed after him, flying in tight formation. High overhead, a lone vulture trailed him through the brush, crying forlornly.

Circling the outlying animal pens, Sibatia entered the graveyard from the south. Weaving between mounds of dirt and stone, he snagged a small hand-carved amulet from one fresh grave and a halfway decent candle stub from another.

Under the earth, the congregation of dead watched everything. They watched each other, they watched him, they watched the cloudless sky. Reaching Meru's plot, Sibatia walked directly across it, scuffing his heels in the dirt.

It had been a while since he'd last visited out here. He'd been neglecting his mother of late. To tell the truth, he was feeling more than a little guilty as he knelt at her grave, hanging the amulet on the marking stake and placing the candle at its base.

Removing the plate-sized rock resting at the head of the grave, Sibatia exposed a smooth-walled hole. Craning forward, he peered down into it for a moment, cocking his head to one side to listen carefully.

"Hello, Ma," he said. "It's me."

Stationing himself atop the neighboring mound, Pudzo started digging away.

"Ma?" Sibatia said again, pressing his lips to the hole, trying to make light of it, but wondering to himself if this might be the time she was finally gone. "You in there?"

Listening again, he thought he caught a faint grunting sound and then a rustling like dry leaves. What, she wasn't alone? Mixing it up maybe with a friendly gentleman caller?

Wait a second. Hold on . . . Could that old fuckhead Meru be down there with her?

63

No way. Not in a million years. Don't even think about it.

Checking to be sure nobody was putzing around nearby, Sibatia took the scrap of Auntie meat out of his pocket and slid it into the hole. Moving back so that his shadow didn't block the opening, he let her have some sun. As an afterthought, he opened his cigarette pouch and removed two Stuyvesants, dropping them both down the hole as well.

"It's all set, Ma," he said, leaning over her once more. "What I had planned? With the Angel, and all? Remember?"

He listened closely, but there wasn't anything to hear.

"Well, that American girl, you know, the one I told you about? It turns out she's very nice, Ma. Very sweet. I think you'd like her, and I know she'd like you."

Again there was no response.

"Are you mad at me or something, Ma?" he asked. "The reason I haven't been coming around much is that I'm awfully busy these days."

Nothing.

All right. All right. Be that way.

I'm not bleeding myself again, thought Sibatia.

Last time, or was it the time before, he'd emptied half his veins down that hole, just to get her to talk.

"Will you fucking knock it off!" he called over to Pudzo. "Quit that damn digging. Now!"

Stretching out over his mother, his head lying beside the opening, Sibatia allowed himself a moment's rest. Almost instantly he dozed off.

Hard again in his shorts, twitching softly in the dirt,

he dreamed he was a Grandfather sweeping low above the Earth, scattering his seed across the fertile plains and great river valleys, dosing entire American cities with his jism.

Wandering over to investigate, Pudzo sniffed suspiciously at the hole, growling quietly as the first muffled sounds of chewing rose from below.

CHAPTER FOUR

1

Charlie had planned on going to the doctor's office with Helen in the morning, but then Helen decided she would rather go alone. If they both went, Molly would know something was up for sure, and Helen didn't want her asking a thousand and one questions. Later, like maybe right after lunch, the three of them would sit down and have a long talk. But until then, the less Molly suspected, the better.

So by nine o'clock, Helen was gone—telling Molly there was an emergency at work—and Charlie was out front washing the RV. Molly had been outside earlier, wandering around the yard, but now she was in taking a shower, rinsing the African dust from her hair.

A bucket, some soap, sponges and rags, the hose unrolled on the driveway and all ready to go—okay, breaktime, Charlie figured, taking the *Motorhome* out of his back pocket and sitting down on the metal step under the Winnebago's side door, the step creaking some with his weight.

Full-time RVing, the magazine's cover said. *Life on the Open Road.*

A Dream Machine forty-footer was parked underneath the words, a real dreadnought built by Lazy Daze. Hell, anybody could live in one of those year-round, Charlie thought. Why would you need a house?

Flipping through the magazine, he shook his head over the glossy photographs of high-tech cockpits and fully-equipped kitchens with oak parquet floors; the living areas with matching fold-out sofas, wet bars, and state-of-the-art audio and video components; the plush designer bedrooms with walk-around queen-size beds and built-in closets.

"Christ Almighty," he mumbled, scanning the measurements of this month's centerfold, the Wanderlodge 42, packing a standard 35,000 BTU electronic-ignition furnace, a two-compressor 24,500 BTU ceiling-ducted Coleman central air conditioner, a 15KW Onan diesel generator and a 2,500-watt inverter—*plus* optional roof-mounted solar panels.

Solar panels?

Why would you ever need a house?

Insulated bays with fully laminated one-piece fiberglass sidewalls, two inches thick. Semi-monocoque steel cage structure for bridgelike stability.

Someday, Charlie told himself. Someday.

He stood and opened the Winnebago's flimsy metal door, tossing the magazine inside. "Come on out of there," he said when he saw Harley lying on the carpet behind the driver's seat. "How'd you get in there?"

Grabbing the hose, Charlie started wetting the RV down, taking his time, rainbows forming in the fine misty spray. Fifteen years old, this baby left a lot to be desired, but how could he complain? He knew a dozen guys at least who'd love to have a twenty-foot Chieftain like this sitting in their driveway.

He was soaping it up when Molly appeared, all fresh and clean from her shower. "Need some help?" she asked.

"There's another sponge in that bucket."

They went at it side by side, moving right along, Molly up on the stepladder going after the higher parts, scrubbing away, the suds soaking her baggy cutoffs and T-shirt. Watching her work, Charlie thought she seemed a lot more like her old self this morning. Still as skinny as hell, sure, but Helen's cooking would take care of that soon enough.

"Once we get this done," he kidded her, "we'll get started on rebuilding that garage roof."

"I say we go for a little spin." She dropped her sponge into the bucket and pushed back a stray lock of hair, leaving a soapy smear across her forehead. "You're probably not going to believe this, but while I was over in Mali, I thought about how we used to cruise around in this old thing, all the time."

"It's not that old," Charlie said.

"How about if we go out to Sherman's Pond or someplace?" Molly suggested. "Or up Route 100 a ways, say to Hogback?"

Why not?

"Sure, I guess we could do that." Charlie thought about waiting until Helen got home from the doctor's, but chances were she wouldn't want to come along with them anyway. "Let's just finish up the back end here, rinse her off, and then we'll go."

"Good deal."

They were done in another fifteen minutes, the RV

sparkling, even the rusty spots looking clean. Molly went inside to leave a note for Helen, while Charlie rewound the hose and put the ladder away in the garage. Climbing behind the wheel of the Winnebago, he took a look in the back, the galley with the stainless-steel sink and hand-pump faucet, the 3x3 refrigerator and double-burner stove, the dinette area's wall-mounted Formica table and twin-anchored chairs.

Yes sir, your basic Class A interior appointments. Charmingly luxurious, to say the least.

The side door slammed open and Harley leapt in, wet feet tracking the carpet as his tail thumped against the cabinets. Molly was right behind him, closing the door and then climbing up front between the seats, the scent of her freshly shampooed hair filling the cab.

"You know," Charlie said, "what you ought to do is find a job in South America when you're finished with nursing school. Like in Brazil, say. That way your mother and I could drive on down to visit you whenever we wanted."

"I don't think there's too many KOA campgrounds along the Amazon, Dad."

"Okay, so we'll rough it."

Charlie turned the key and hit the gas, coaxing the engine into a smooth idle. Taking a tissue from the box on the dashboard, he gave the PILOT sign taped in front of the steering wheel a few quick swipes, cleaning off the dust.

"By the way, we're going up to the cabin the weekend after next, maybe to stay a whole week. How about coming along with us?"

"You driving this thing up?"

"Hell, don't we always?" Putting the RV in reverse, Charlie backed it out of the driveway, taking it slow. "Actually, you could follow us in the car, and then leave whenever you wanted to, say in the middle of the week. I mean, if you didn't feel like staying the entire time."

"To tell you the truth, Daddy, I wouldn't mind heading up there today."

"Yeah, me neither. The lake's nice and warm, and I'm sure the fish are biting like crazy. They're probably lined up in rows, waiting for me."

"So? Let's do it."

It sure was tempting. "I wish we could, honey," he finally said. "But I guess we'll just have to wait."

Molly shrugged and smiled, then rolled the window down, the wind blowing her hair around as the RV picked up some speed.

Good old Molly, she'll never change, Charlie thought. Even when she was just a kid, she was always ready to drop everything and go.

When they reached the pond, there were no cars at all in the lower lot, but they followed the shore around to the far side anyway, and parked there.

The instant Molly opened her door, Harley jumped out and took off after some ducks napping along the water's edge. He'd been chasing birds his entire life, but he'd never come close to catching one yet, and this time was no different. The ducks scrambled away to safety, winging hard, and Harley had to settle for sending a few barks after them—*I'll get you! I'll get you! I'll get! You!*—the sound echoing off the surrounding hills.

70

"Hey, boy, how about this?" Molly said, taking a small black ball from her pants pocket. When she threw it out into the water, Harley dove right in, the air blowing from his cheeks as he swam along.

There was no sign of anyone else around the pond. Charlie kicked himself for not bringing his pole. Last time he'd been out here, he'd caught three brown trout in less than half an hour. The pond wasn't all that big, but it shelved off nicely into unknown depths, and it was clear year-round.

"We should've brought our poles along with us," he said, "and done a little fishing. Just for old times' sake, you know?"

"Yeah, we should've."

When Harley came bounding out of the water, Molly took the ball from him but didn't throw it again. Harley sat waiting for a moment, then shook himself dry and wandered off.

"Hey, look." Molly pointed ahead toward the south end of the pond where a thick stand of tall evergreens shadowed the shore. "A beaver house."

"Sure is," Charlie agreed. "Let's go take a look."

Charlie had checked it out the last time around, and had pretty much decided then that it was abandoned. He hadn't seen a single piece of freshly chewed wood anywhere near the igloo, the skinned poles all seasoned silver and gray.

Catching a scent, Harley put his nose to the ground and peeled away to the left, loping up the hill and disappearing behind an outcropping of rock.

"Raccoon," Charlie remarked. "Or deer."

Down along the shore, where a dozen white birches leaned out over the dark water, a bullfrog called hoarsely from a thick patch of pickerel weed and arrowhead. *Be drowned . . . drowned . . . be drowned.* Two dragonflies went zipping by, one fire-colored and the other cobalt-blue, chasing their reflections across the mirror-still surface of the pond.

"In Mali, they call those things flying needles," Molly said, watching them go. "Mothers tell their kids that if they're naughty, they'll come at night and sew up their eyes."

"That's a nice thing to say to a little kid." Shaking his head, Charlie looked out toward the center of the pond just in time to see a good-size bass leap clear and come down in a silvery splash.

"Yeah, you should've brought along those poles, Dad," Molly said, juggling the black ball from one hand to the other.

"Don't I know it."

"Well, we'll get him next time," she added quietly, letting her arms drop to her sides. "Right?"

"Damn right," Charlie agreed.

Next time . . . Man, that sounded great.

It was still hard to believe that there was an entire year waiting ahead of them, while Molly attended nursing school. A whole wonderful year to go fishing together—summer, winter, spring, you name it.

Of course, next August she'd be leaving again, heading back to Africa most likely, but there was no sense even thinking about that now.

"Hey, Daddy? I want to ask you something," Molly said, coming over to stand beside him. "And I want you to tell me the truth, okay?"

"Sure." Charlie bent down and picked up a handful of stones, knowing what was coming.

72

"Mom's worse, isn't she?" Molly took a deep breath and sighed. "I mean, a lot worse."

Charlie sent one of the stones skipping away toward the opposite shore.

"Yeah, she is," he finally said. "She's been meaning to talk to you about it, you know, but I guess she just doesn't want you to worry. Hell, sometimes I wonder if she tells me half of what's going on."

"Is the cancer spreading?"

Charlie tossed another stone. It skipped once and sank from sight, gone in an instant.

"They say maybe it's moving into her hip. How bad, they don't know exactly, at least not yet." He lobbed the rest of the stones out into the water, one by one. "But your being home now and all, I'm sure that'll help keep her spirits up. And that's the important thing, honey, right there. Keeping her mind off it, as much as possible anyway, so that she doesn't dwell on it constantly."

Molly reached over then and touched his arm. There was a short silence.

"Don't you worry, Daddy," she said, her voice soft and soothing. "You'll see. Everything's going to be just fine."

"Well, I hope so," Charlie told her. "I sure hope so."

And that's when it happened.

Without warning, Molly shut her eyes and tipped her head back, bringing her hands up in front of her, clutching the shiny black ball to her chest. She stayed that way for a moment, and then she made a noise like a horse, a strange, unsettling huffing sound, her mouth falling open and her tongue lolling.

"Molly?" Charlie said in alarm, taking a step toward her. "Molly, what is it? What's wrong?"

She began to shake and tremble, every muscle in her body quivering. Christ, she's having a seizure! Charlie realized.

But then she seemed to snap out of it, her eyes clear and calm once again as she stepped forward to embrace him.

Grabbing him around the waist, she effortlessly pulled him to the ground, kicking his feet out from under him. Too astonished to react, Charlie fell flat on his back and she quickly crawled onto him, straddling his chest and pinning his arms with her knees.

When he tried to free himself, she leaned forward and held his shoulders down. He struggled for a moment, but it was useless. She wasn't even straining, and yet he could hardly move. How could she be so strong?

Planting his feet, he twisted frantically from side to side, attempting to throw her off. She was sobbing now, gazing down at him, her tears falling onto his chest.

"Molly!" he cried out. *"Jesus!"*

And then she did it.

Gripping his jaw firmly with one hand, she put the black ball into his mouth, cramming her fist between his teeth. Gagging, Charlie thrashed desperately beneath her, trying to shout. Molly grunted and thrust her hand deeper still, and suddenly Charlie could no longer breathe.

Panicking, his vision beginning to swim, he kicked and writhed, but her hold was relentless. Lowering her face, she snatched her fist out of his mouth and clamped his jaw shut, her hands bone-cold against his skin.

"Don't worry, Daddy," she told him, her eyes full of sparkling tears. "Everything's going to be fine. You'll see."

Charlie felt the ball pushing against the back of his throat. He began to black out, his chest heaving as he choked. His mind blind with shock, he made one final attempt to fight her off. But it was hopeless, the last of his strength was gone.

"I love you, Daddy," Molly said quietly. She leaned forward and gently kissed his brow.

Everything seemed to pause. The world darkened and turned a queasy red. Charlie felt his daughter kiss him a second time, and then the thing in his throat shivered and slid deeper.

2

In the place where the Red Uncles dwell, on the borders of the measureless Void, there was once a young woman who cried constantly for food. She had mouths in her wrists, mouths under her arms, a mouth in each breast, and even one between her legs.

"She can't live here," the Uncles said, touching their members together in consultation. "She will have to go somewhere else."

But in those black days, the world had not yet been created. It existed merely in the shape of Nothingness, unperceived and unattainable, wholly immersed in a dream. Up above, there was only the empty air, and in front and behind it was exactly the same. Limitless, quiescent, unchanging. Nevertheless, there was an immense mass far below that might have been heaped-up water. Or blood. Where it had come from, no one recalled.

If we put her down there, the Uncles thought, perhaps she will no longer be hungry.

So they seized her and carried her below, but she simply begged louder than ever. She spat on the water, and struck it and churned it, causing great defluxions and torrents that shook the Void's foundations.

When they saw how she behaved, the Red Uncles grew angry, and pulling on her limbs from all four directions, they tore her into many pieces.

"Now what?" they asked.

Not knowing what else to do, they used her to make the world, assigning a name and form to everything, such was their might.

They created grass and flowers from her hair, and from her bones and marrow they made the forests. From her eyes they devised lakes and ponds, and from her breasts they fashioned the hills. From her golden flesh the first vast deserts were forged, her veins forming swift rivers and streams. Her breath became the wind and the clouds, and the insects creeping over her body became human beings. Lunar mansions for the wisest sages were constructed from her chaste womb.

At last, she will be satisfied, the Red Uncles thought.

But just as before, her mouths were lurking everywhere, always snapping open and shut, forever moaning and begging. Forever hungry.

When it rains, she drinks. When someone dies, she eats. Yet her mouths are never filled.

Sometimes, if you listen closely, you can still hear her crying . . .

As the RV pulled into the driveway, it bucked violently and then stalled, the front bumper clipping her parents' new car and pushing it forward into the garage door. Hands clutching the wheel, Molly sat there for a moment, her mind going back and forth like a lion pacing in a filthy cage.

Tipping her head forward, she struggled briefly and brought up another seed, vomiting it out into her cupped palms. Sparkling with an eerie space-black glimmer, a cool gelatin glow that seemed to come from within, the tiny sphere trembled softly in her hands.

From the rear of the RV her father groaned, stirring on the floor. Sitting close beside him, Harley looked up at Molly and whined.

The gods ride on the back of all men, she reminded herself. And none can ever be rid of them. But seeing her poor father lying there so helplessly, Molly felt a dark and terrible chill go skating through her soul.

Climbing out of the Winnebago, she walked slowly across the lawn, mounting the front steps just as her mother appeared behind the screen door, an expression of shock locked onto her face.

"Molly? What is it?"

And it was right then, at that very instant, that Molly heard the Hungry Woman's cry—a keening wail of pure despair, rising from the heart of this black world—there for only a moment, and then gone.

When she kicked the door open, it struck her mother squarely on the forehead and sent her reeling back into the house, her arms windmilling as she did a drunken two-step and fell to the carpet. Moving quickly now, with an almost mechanical swiftness, Molly dropped to her knees and circled her mother's throat with one arm, pressing the seed firmly against her lips.

"Don't fight me, Mom," she said, forcing herself to speak quietly, calmly. "Just don't fight me, okay?"

Her mother let out a broken moan, her eyes bulging wide with uncomprehending horror. Before she could say anything, Molly jammed the black seed home, tightening her grip around her mother's thin neck as she kicked and flailed. The moment her mother swallowed, Molly closed her eyes so that she wouldn't have to see any more.

The sound of her racing heart, the movement of her blood pulsing . . . she felt like she was in a vacuum, unable to take in air. When her mother finally went slack, Molly relaxed her hold, letting the frail gray head fall onto her lap.

The old woman twitched quietly, her fingers plucking at nothing, her heels lightly drumming the floor. She pissed herself, then defecated as well. Molly reached down and brushed the hair away from her face, using a sleeve to wipe the drool pooling from the corner of her mouth.

Eventually, her mother shuddered and sighed, entering her dreams, dreams of bounty and haven. Dreams of peace. In a hushed voice, Molly began to softly hum, the lullaby's haunting melody eliciting one last convulsive spasm from the old woman's frame.

Attracted by the song, the lizard poked its head out of Molly's bedroom, then came jittering down the hallway. As it stood before her with its eyes closed, swaying to the sound of her voice, Molly felt the remainder of the seeds stirring within her belly, each patiently awaiting its turn.

Sometime later, regaining her strength, Molly went outside for some air. Stripping off her clothes, she dove into the pool, but climbed right out again after only a few laps. Stealing a handful of cherry tomatoes from the garden, she ate them one by one, then walked over to the old maple tree in the center of the yard.

Gripping the lowest branch, she hoisted herself onto it, first kneeling and then standing upright. She continued to climb, doing so without difficulty, moving confidently from limb to limb as the tree came alive around her.

Bands of polished sunlight rippled through the myriad leaves, a radiant, prismatic glow that transformed her bare flesh into a brilliant mosaic of colors. Fractal rainbows spangled the air, flickering like jeweled mandalas.

Ascending steadily into the stained-glass canopy, Molly thought of her parents. She remembered how her father had smiled at her as she stepped off the bus yesterday, and how her mother had gathered her in such a warm embrace, welcoming her home. She thought of the three of them together in the kitchen last night, the smell of her mother's lasagna filling the house. She thought of her mother, so weak and frail, lying on the living room floor, and she began to cry.

She cried for her parents and she cried for herself. They had each lived their own lives in this world, sometimes together and sometimes alone, and now the world was about to swallow them all.

Shutting her eyes, pressing her cheek against the trunk of the tree, Molly rested for a moment, tired and winded from her climb. Overhead, beyond the crazy sprawl of limbs above her, she could hear something moving about. An instant later a giant red bird swooped down, clutching a shredded chunk of some nameless black meat. Alighting on a nearby branch, it fixed her with a knowing stare. From its delicate wings and elongated, nearly featherless body, it was clear that it had come from the tree's higher reaches.

From way up deep where the air was thinner, Molly thought, beginning to climb once again.

From the place where the Red Uncles dwell . . .

CHAPTER FIVE

The heavy, tired sun had slanted down and finally fallen from the sky. Floating just above the town, the first hungry stars revealed themselves, the weaker ones moving closer every night, almost near enough now to hear.

Working things around in his head, Sibatia went up one street and down the next. Outside the blacksmith's shop, three drunken young soldiers, Kamaras from the north, flicked their cigarettes at him and offered to escort him down to the river.

"Come on, wild man." They laughed, fondling their crotches. "One date with us, and you will find your hidden heart."

Everyone else in the village ignored him, however, same as they always did, blank eyes drifting right over him as if he were just a dog turd lying in the road.

Well, fuck them all. After tomorrow, or the next day, whatever—they'd be talking about him for years to come. Little boys would be afraid to play in the bush, and men would keep their knives good and sharp. Girls would have trouble sleeping at night, and women would take to wandering alone through the fields.

At the south end of town he found what he was looking for, a family of sorts—a woman in her early twenties, her belly big with child, a small boy three or four years old lying beside her on the ground, his head resting in the lap of an ancient crone, the woman's grandmother no doubt—up-country refugees on their merry way to the capital, fleeing the drought.

The gnarled old woman spotted him first, her mouth warped in a scowl as her stare locked onto his. The young woman was leaning back against a tree, her eyes remaining closed as he approached.

"Pardon me," Sibatia said, greeting her with a friendly smile, startling her awake. "I couldn't help but notice . . ."

A single dirty blanket, a pot, an empty plastic water jug. The old woman clutched a chicken under her arm, a diseased, featherless creature. The boy's belly was slightly swollen by hunger, while the young woman's was impossibly large, large enough to be carrying a bush hog.

Sibatia smiled again, gesturing hesitantly toward it all.

"I don't wish to offend," he continued, concern slipping into his voice. "However . . . I would like to offer my help."

When people become sufficiently desperate, they'll do just about anything. Steal, fight, even trust someone like him.

The weariness in the young woman's face was searing. She'd seen enough grief and madness to last several lifetimes.

"I do not have much, but . . . perhaps a small

82

meal?" Sibatia suggested. "The boy, eh? He would like some rice?"

Casting a warding sign at Sibatia with her thumb and little finger, the old woman craned forward and snatched up a stick lying beside her legs. Bobbing her head, she started scratching something in the dust.

"I live nearby," Sibatia persisted, pointing farther along the street. "Right over there."

The young woman turned to look, ignoring the grandmother.

"Mommy, I'm hungry," the boy said listlessly, and that seemed to settle the matter. The young woman nodded to Sibatia, quickly, as if afraid he might change his mind, Sibatia thinking, *Techniques and mystiques.* Thinking, *Maybe I should get a job with the U-fucking-N.*

"You see?" Shrugging amiably, he glanced down at the boy and then back at the mother. "A little hot soup, okay?"

There never really was a question that she would come with him. If there had been, he wouldn't have stopped to speak with her in the first place.

Without saying a word, she prodded the boy with her finger, and then stood. Gathering their belongings in her arms, she continued to ignore the old woman, who was still scratching busily in the dirt.

"What's your name?" Sibatia asked the boy as he climbed to his feet.

"He is called Tokpa," the mother replied. "He turned six only last week. He is my son."

Poor little stunted bastard, Sibatia thought. To the north, the valleys were filling with bones, the rivers thick with corpses floating downstream.

"Mother Koli, we must go," the young woman said, addressing the crone at last. "This man—"

"Sibatia."

"—Sibatia, has kindly offered to help us."

In the northern hills, the nights were red with burning villages. At dawn, vultures darkened the sky.

When Sibatia stepped forward to give the old fart a hand up, she recoiled from him with a choking squawk, the chicken lunging toward his outstretched fingers, beak stabbing the air.

"Mother Koli." The young woman was too exhausted to be angry. "Excuse her, please. She is not herself. The last few days—"

"I understand," Sibatia hastened to assure her. "No need to explain."

On her feet now, the old woman fixed her beady chicken eyes on him, a chill gleam lighting her nutbrown face.

"When Uncle is in the forest," she hissed fiercely, jabbing the broken stick toward the ground, "even the spiders hide."

Well, well, what do we have here? Sibatia wondered, glancing down at the stylized skull the crone had scratched into the dirt. Don't tell me this senile old lizard is some sort of witch.

How quaint.

"Please, Mother Koli," the young woman tried again, pressing the blanket, jug, and pot against her belly. "For Tokpa's sake."

Reaching out, Sibatia took the pan and plastic jug from her, offering her a sympathetic smile.

"Perhaps if we simply start walking—sorry, what is your name?"

"Yolanda. Yolanda Matomb."

"Ah, yes, Yolanda . . . My home is not far at all. A minute or two, no more."

Let's go, you stupid sow, Sibatia thought impatiently. It's time to kiss this miserable life of yours goodbye.

"My wife is most likely nearly through preparing supper," he added. "She is not the world's best cook, but . . ." All right, enough already. ". . . but still, we try to help people whenever we can."

As always, hunger won out in the end. Yolanda grasped her son's hand. "Her feet are very sore," she said apologetically, gesturing toward the old woman. "Mother Koli? Did you hear? It is not far, where we are going."

"Sitting quietly reveals crocodile's tricks," the crazy hag whispered scornfully to the chicken in her arms. "I know him."

Clucking nervously, the bird seemed to be alarmed at the news.

"This way, please," Sibatia said, masking his amusement. Stepping aside, he purposefully scuffed his heel across Uncle's portrait in the dirt. "But wait. Perhaps you would prefer it if I simply brought you something here instead. Yes?"

That did it. At this point, Yolanda wasn't about to settle for sharing a bowl of lukewarm rice along the roadside.

"One moment," she said, giving Sibatia a pleading, dewy-eyed look. "Let me speak with her."

Obligingly, Sibatia withdrew, walking down the road several paces, her melancholy innocence igniting a small flare of anticipation in his loins.

* * *

"Apparently, the wife has stepped out," Sibatia told his guests, shutting the front door of Tembro's hut behind them. "But look, she's left us our supper."

With their attention fixed squarely upon the table, Sibatia ushered them each into a seat. Slipping a cushion under the young child and politely pushing in Yolanda's chair, he let the crone alone.

Palm butter and rice, cassava and cold rabbit. He poured them each a cup of cane juice and passed around a bowl of koala nuts. They ate like soldiers attacking their first hot meal after a week in the field. Even the chicken couldn't stop chowing it down.

Good thing Meru had enough foresight to lay aside such a sizable stash. Sibatia hated to waste so much food on these people, but it was the easiest way he could think of to get them all to take their medicine, the *come along* and the *seed strengthener,* the *Auntie's pee* for purity, and of course the *brain wash.*

Rule number one: Never put on airs while entertaining.

"I'll just step over to the neighbor's and see if the wife's there," he told them, opening the back door. "I won't be a minute."

He found Tembro sitting on a stool in the middle of the yard. Lighting a Stuyvesant, Sibatia stood beside him for a moment, glad to be away from the refugees.

Curled in Tembro's lap, the infant was motionless, sleeping perhaps, the wound in Tembro's breast like a dead man's smile. White flies by the score swarmed around his natty hair and shoulders, coasting in for landings and launching off again, all in perfect silence. Overhead, stars were falling like confetti as the full moon climbed above the trees.

"Kill me, Uncle," Tembro murmured quietly, turning his blind gaze skyward. "I beg you."

The baby's flesh was cool and soft, soft as a dream. Tenderly, Sibatia brushed his fingertips along its tiny delicate spine. When he put his cigarette out against its buttocks, it stirred sleepily and resumed sucking at Tembro's wound.

Returning inside, he was relieved to see that the various potions had taken effect. Yolanda, her son, the old witch—all three of them were lolling at the table now like lobotomized zombies, mannequins on the nod.

Too much *brain wash?*

For an instant Sibatia imagined a different life for himself, the village *mganga* returning home after a busy day, his loving wife, child, and mother-in-law waiting patiently to share their evening meal.

But what's this? Why, the family pet seemed a tad ill. Something it ate, perhaps?

Crumpled on the floor at the old lady's feet, the bald scabby chicken was twitching like a spastic fish.

Hey, don't you worry, kids. Mega*mganga* will take care of everything.

Bending down, Sibatia scooped up the bird and put an end to its suffering, twisting his fists until its scrawny neck went snap, crackle, pop.

Whoever said he didn't have a size-ten heart?

It was after midnight when they finally set out. Keeping to the side streets and back alleys, they left the village unseen, circling through the moonlit fields to the sacred grove.

As was only natural following such a respected

shaman's death, it would be quite a while before anyone dared to set foot in the grove, for fear of disturbing Meru's spirit. The day of the funeral, the place had been busy enough—especially after the discovery of poor Isaak's corpse—but once Meru had been properly laid to rest, the grove had been declared off-limits until the next new moon.

Pure hoodoo bullshit, of course, but awfully convenient as far as Sibatia was concerned.

"Hey there, boy," he said, greeting Pudzo at the break in the hedge. "See any spooks?"

When the old crone came to a limping halt, Pudzo growled at her for a moment, then walked over and pissed on her leg.

"Here you go." Sibatia laughed, prying the dead chicken from the woman's arms. Swinging it above his head, he tossed it into the trees, Pudzo chasing it down and snagging it on the second bounce.

"Beautiful animal, eh?" Sibatia remarked to Yolanda. "I taught him everything he knows."

She had a slap-happy smile on her face, but her eyes held nothing except fear. Transfixed, she stared back at him like a mesmerized hare caught in the headlights of an onrushing car. Making a helpless gesture of resignation, she finally turned and started shuffling down the path, dragging the boy behind her.

"Let's go, Grandma," Sibatia said, giving the stupefied old harridan a shove. "Just between you and me, that little lady sets my nectar flowing."

They left the path before reaching Meru's hut, Sibatia leading his guests through the woods, carrying the boy the last thirty meters or so, up on his shoulders the way his grandpa had often carried him.

"Don't worry, kid," he told the softly sobbing boy.

"I've got you. You won't fall. Just don't muss my hair, okay?"

When they reached the black gum tree, Pudzo was already busy with the two old men Sibatia had found camped along the river that morning—Nathan and Ken Nobambo, brothers no less—smokeheads with no more sense than a pair of balls. The dog was licking at the sac of pus pillowing out of the bottom guy's back.

In a silver pool of moonlight, the germinus sat, a sofa-sized mound of mutated tissue and fruiting gristle. Bloated florets of pulpy flesh rose from the spongy mass, emitting the summery stench of sour meat. Gaily animated tendrils as pale as embryos pulsed in the charged air, rillets of creamy fluid seeping from their fluted tips. Amidst it all lay the two old coots.

"Get the hell outta there," Sibatia told the dog.

Lifting his lips in a silent snarl, Pudzo hopped off the pile, retrieved his chicken, and strolled over to a patch of moon shadow.

Setting the boy down, Sibatia took a closer look at the thing at the base of the tree. When one of the men embedded in the burbling mound snapped open his eyes, Sibatia nodded a friendly hello.

"God, it's all such a surprise, isn't it?" he said, addressing both Yolanda and the old men.

When Yolanda let out a slurred guttural groan, Sibatia lifted his hands and shrugged. "Okay, it's not much so far, I admit. But it's a start."

Going over to the tree, he took down the pouch hanging from the lowest branch. "Time for dessert," he told the old woman, fishing two seeds out of the bag.

Using his pocketknife—all right, Meru's pocketknife—he carefully punctured the small spheres a half-dozen times each, thinking maybe he should expedite things by opening Granny up as well.

"Body of Uncle, body of Uncle," he recited, getting a good grip on the witchy old lady and shoving the first seed into her toothless mouth.

Stunned awake, she surfaced from her trance for one harrowing instant, just long enough to utter a few words.

"I know you . . . I've seen you in my dreams."

"You and nine zillion other people, Grandma," Sibatia told her, sliding the second seed down her throat. "If you bite me, you'll be eating your teeth next."

With a deft twist he worked her neck around until it made the same exact sound as the chicken's. Dropping her to the ground, he had her clothes off before her eyes even misted over.

"I'll be damned," he said, seeing the faded, hand-sized tree tattooed on her wrinkly belly.

Maybe she did know him after all.

Carrying her over to the mound, Sibatia heaved her up on top, the Nobambo brothers shifting slightly to accommodate her, a globose bulb of syrupy pureed hash bursting beneath her weight as she settled deeper into the dark, mucousy mass.

The boy was next. He had some trouble with his seeds, but he was a hungry little guy, and he eventually swallowed them both down. Stripping off his dirty shorts and ragged T-shirt, Sibatia felt his heart jerk up a notch at the sight of the kid's bone-thin legs and fat doll-like tummy.

"Don't worry, champ," he told the boy, tempering his voice. "Being an angel isn't so bad."

When he set him on the mound, the son of a gun actually gave him a small smile, as Nathan Nobambo reached out a viscous arm to embrace him.

"Fine boy you have there," Sibatia told Yolanda. "Call me a sentimental fool, if you will, but you should be mighty proud of him."

Her face was twisted into a tortured grimace, but her eyes were vacant and clear. She made a snorting, snaffling sound as Sibatia disrobed her, removing her threadbare raffia skirt and blouse, her soiled undergarments, her cheap shiny earrings and the necklace of chimpanzee teeth hanging between her milk-heavy breasts.

He turned her around admiringly, naked in the bright silver moonlight, her great round belly abloom with sores and boils.

"Please," she whispered pathetically as he selected two seeds from his pouch. "Please . . ."

"Now, now," he told her, making a mental note to up the dosage of *come along* next time. Leaning forward, he licked the tears off her pretty face. "Spare me the heartbreak, okay? It'll just give me gas."

As he fed her the seeds, she struggled and whined, but not too stridently, no doubt because her kid was watching, his head and shoulders still unabsorbed.

"There, that wasn't so terrible, was it?" he asked once both seeds were down.

Moving her closer to the mound, he forced her to bend at the waist, then circled around behind her and grabbed her firmly by the hips. Pressing against her ass, taking his time, he walked her slowly forward, until the mound sucked her in right up to her belly.

Stepping back, he watched her do a little dance, her

buttocks bucking some as the whole structure shivered gently, coming alive to welcome her.

Turning away, Sibatia nearly tripped over the chicken. Busy grooming himself in the moonlight, Pudzo had only eaten the bird's head. Bending down, Sibatia took the thing and tossed it onto the pile.

CHAPTER SIX

———

1

Welcome to Wal-Mart," the greeter said as Molly entered the store. "How are you this evening?"

You live for sixty, sixty-five years, an entire lifetime, and then you end up standing here for eight hours a day, five days a week, smiling at every schmuck who walks into the store. Christ, talk about bad karma. You had to wonder exactly what this old guy did in his former life to deserve a fate like this.

"Well, I'm feeling better, thanks," Molly told him. "I haven't passed much blood at all today."

"Lucky you," the old duffer pronounced, already turning toward the next customer. "Hi, there. Welcome to Wal-Mart."

God, all these wonderful colors. Walking deeper into the store, Molly's eyes widened, trying to take everything in. It was unreal how bright and clear this place was. Cartoon bright. Space-station bright.

The sound of a thousand violins shifted down from the pure white ceiling above, "Raindrops Keep Falling on My Head," right? Shoppers glided by on either side, pushing their shiny, merchandise-ladened carts, searching every aisle diligently for bargains. Happy uniformed workers, courteous drones forever ready with a pleasant smile, restocked the shelves and chatted amiably among themselves.

What a terrific store, Molly thought, pausing to savor the scene. If you ever needed a place to go insane, this was it. Veering left, she grabbed a bag of Skittles from a display bin, a fun-size package, *Come on and taste the rainbow!*

Every town should have a Wal-Mart.

"Security scan, department ten, please," a woman's voice announced on the speakers overhead. "Security scan, department ten. Thank you."

Ripping the package open, Molly emptied it into one of the many pockets of her Army jacket, crumpling the wrapper and tossing it away.

PETS AND HOBBIES. AUTOMOTIVE CENTER. HEALTH AND BEAUTY.

Miles of aisles. Where to first?

Munching on a handful of candy, she turned right and headed for KITCHENWARE.

Mixers and dicers, shooters and juicers. A four-slice toaster with a Mastermind heat/moisture sensor, only $29.95. A Sahara food dehydrator-blender deal, featuring a unique thermo-siphoning system. *As seen on TV!*

And on sale this week only, a whole row of monster 1000-watt microwave ovens—recommended lead-filled apron not included—a young long-haired couple in jeans and matching denim jackets standing before the largest unit of them all, smiling and fiddling with the computerized control panel, dreaming of the good life to come.

At the end of the aisle Molly selected a seven-inch Chef kitchen knife, going with the cherrywood handle rather than the black polysteel. Opening the package, she slipped the knife free and tested the never-needs-sharpening blade against her palm, leaving a bright ribbon of blood across her flesh.

Cartoon bright.

Chef! The finest in cutlery!

When she looked up, she caught the long-haired guy giving her the eye. Running her tongue along her lips, she smiled and pointedly dropped her gaze, fixing it on the crotch of his pants. Coquettishly, she reached down and touched herself between her legs, wincing slightly as she rubbed her wound.

When she glanced back up, he was standing closer to his wife, sneaking furtive peeks at her like a nervous little boy, a broken distance in his eyes. When she licked her bloody hand, he turned away for good.

"Marv, 203, please. Marv, 203," said a loud voice in the ceiling, a different voice than the one before. "Thank you."

Sliding the knife into her pocket, Molly moved along. As she strolled through Home Furnishings, she took out her keys and left a nice gouge in the center of several coffee tables and desktops. Halfway down the empty mirror aisle, she was suddenly surrounded by a crowd of very familiar strangers.

The Beatles? Elton John? Something light and sassy was playing on the sound system, one hundred muted trombones doing what? "Penny Lane"?

Ah, TOYS . . .

Baby Burpy, Newborn Cuddle Baby, Little Baby Sleepy, Baby Ca-Ca. Molly snapped the heads off three Baby Get Wells, sticking them inside the oven of the Littlest Cook's kitchen set.

Then came the store's Barbie department, this week's on-sale specials including Glitter Beach Barbie, Great Weekend Barbie, Secret Hearts Barbie, Hollywood Hair Barbie, and the Barbie Bathroom playset, just the place for some fun with Ken.

TRY ME! it said on the Etch-A-Sketch. So Molly did, drawing a tree on the screen, restarting three times before she finally got it right.

Passing two ten-year-old boys studying the G.I. Joe shelves, she offered them each a bloody handful of candy. When they refused, she crammed a Skittle into her left nostril and snorted it in.

Come on and taste the rainbow!

Selecting a black marker from the art supplies rack, she scrawled a skull onto every globe sitting on the shelf, a dark glaring death's-head centered smack on Mali.

"Someone pick up in Toys, please. Someone pick up in Toys," went the loudspeakers. "Thank you."

Over in HARDWARE, she stole a pair of nine-inch Stanley tongue-and-groove pliers, only $8.97. *Why not the best?* Stopping in HEALTH AND BEAUTY, she opened a box of Tylenol PM extra-strength caplets and poured ten or so into her mouth, pocketing the rest for later.

Security caught up with her right about then, some ex-jock buzz-cut schmo trailing her through INTI-MATES, spy eyes getting all sweaty as she lingered before the silk teddies and skimpy push-up bras, sheer and shimmery with satin trim and matching garters.

Holding a pair of lacy, crotchless panties against her loins, she gave him a little bump-and-grind routine, pretending not to notice him standing at the end of the aisle.

Selecting a Gitano blouse off a nearby rack, she walked over to one of the changing booths. Inside, pulling down her jeans, she took a dump on the bench, a whitish blood-speckled turd as round as an egg, a fine fringe of blue-green filaments sprouting from its crown. Using the blouse to wipe herself, she bent over the bench and inhaled deeply.

Violets, vanilla, sunshine on a field of clover. The rich redolent odor filled her with contentment.

It smelled like Africa.

Returning the soiled blouse to its rack, Molly made her way toward the front of the store, Mr. Security no doubt still following after her, although for the moment she couldn't spot him. Passing through ELECTRONICS—the TVs all playing Rush Limbaugh, thankfully with the volume off—she inserted a handful of Skittles into the most expensive VCR on display. Pausing at a Smith Corona word processor, she thought for a minute, then typed a sentence on the screen.

A TRUE WARRIOR HAS NOTHING TO FEAR FROM THE UNKNOWN

"Excuse me, miss?" the schmo went, finally making his move and grabbing her arm, his smile a dead leer. "Could you come with me, please?"

"Well, this is hardly the place for that," Molly replied straight-faced. "But I'll try if you want me to."

When he tightened his grip, she laughed edgily. "You're out of your tree," she told him.

Easily breaking his hold, she lifted a camcorder off the nearest shelf, a GE 8:1 ultrazoom, featuring a flying erase head, only $399.99. Whirling, she smashed it into his face, blood splashing everywhere as he staggered back against the frieze of Rush Limbaughs and fell sniveling to the floor, eyeballs bouncing in his head.

Plucking the walkie-talkie off his belt, Molly hit the Send button and shoved the thing oh so gently into his broken-toothed mouth.

"Security to ladies changing stalls, please," said the loudspeakers. "Security to ladies changing stalls. Thank you."

Humming along with the zippy Frank Sinatra number drifting down from above, Molly continued toward the front of the store, exiting between two vacant registers. The black glass doors swung open for her with an almost orgasmic sigh as she cruised outside into the starstruck night, joining the dozens of weary brain-dead shoppers milling aimlessly about the parking lot, steering their overflowing carts through the darkness, searching for their cars.

2

Downtown, at the Joshua Tree, perched on the corner stool at the bar, Eddie Starling sipped his beer. Saturday night, ten o'clock, where else would he be?

The crowd was large and the band loud. Eddie had been drinking Millers since six. He had some money left in his pocket, and an idea in his head. Twenty bucks, to be exact, and this: He wanted something different tonight.

He was tired of the usual fare, the cutie girls thirsty for jit, the sweet young things still baby-pink and squeaky. Tempting, sure, but half the time as soon as the real fun got started, they just turned skittish and shy. Which made for some interesting situations—okay, there was no denying that—but tonight Eddie had something else in mind.

Nursing his beer, he watched the TV up on the wall. As near as he could figure, a bunch of old people were trapped on a resort island with some sort of nest of mutant creatures. A *Fantasy Island* meets *Aliens* kind of a deal. The volume was off, but that didn't matter. You more or less knew what everybody was saying anyway.

Just as something was fixing to hatch inside an old lady, Eddie felt a hand squeezing his arm.

"Eddie?" a voice said. "Hey, how ya doing?"

Turning, he saw this all-right-looking girl slipping into focus. Long blond hair, big happy smile—maybe a bit too happy, if you asked him—giving his arm another quick feel as she climbed onto the stool beside him.

"Howdy," Eddie went. "You touch that muscle again, I'm gonna have to charge you."

Up on the TV, the old woman was bursting at the seams. In such cases one does not talk of cure.

"You don't remember me, do you?" the girl said.

Eddie was clueless. She looked familiar, sort of, but no more than anybody else. "I don't like getting into those kind of questions," he told her.

She seemed to think that was funny. When she

ordered a drink, he went with another beer. The band played on, louder than ever, the crowd pressing shoulder to shoulder, ass to ass, everybody doing their best to make the most of this particular night.

She told him her name, but he still couldn't place her. He hadn't the slightest. "Oh yeah," he said, taking the friendly route. "It's all coming back to me now."

She was a little long in the tooth for him, mid-twenties maybe, but she definitely had a decent set of co-ops on her. When she started telling him about Africa, about how she'd been over there for like the last six months, Eddie played along. "Well, well. Live and learn."

After a while he had to drain the dragon. She promised to save him his seat. In the john, though, a joint was going around, and one thing led to another. He was thinking she'd be gone by the time he finally got back, but she was still right there, with a fresh beer waiting for him on the bar.

"I heard somewhere that lions in Africa like to screw for hours," he said. "I think it might've been on *Jeopardy.*"

"Lions, elephants, zebras, apes." She poked him in the ribs, like she was testing a side of beef. "It's something in the air," she told him, giving him that go-for-it smile again. "It's contagious."

Eddie's heart went all yearny. A laugh jerked deep inside him. Anything else I should know?

Suddenly, the night was still young. Up on the TV, the creatures began to feed.

He followed her in his car. He was low on gas, but this way he could leave whenever he felt like it. He'd give her a good pumping, straighten her spine some, then see what was what. Maybe he'd head back to the bar, or stick around her place and look at her slides from the Congo. Her parents were supposedly away for the weekend, so there was definitely potential here. A hunter whc does not take risks, he reminded himself, is no hunter at all.

Okay, okay. He was ready for something like this.

Except for the gas. She was taking him out to the boonies, out River Road toward Putney and who the fuck knows where else, with the needle on E. If he ended up parked next to some cow, he was gonna be pissed.

Good thing he'd brought a six-pack before setting out on this odyssey. Chucking an empty out the window, he snuck another look down at the fuel gauge, thinking maybe he should've gotten two sixes. When she finally pulled into the driveway, he screeched the brakes a little as he coasted in right behind her, his elbow accidently sounding the horn as hc climbed from the car.

"You didn't tell me we were driving halfway back to Africa," he said, opening another beer. "Where the hell are we? Canada?"

The housc was dark, the stars bright and closc overhead, a soft breeze rustling the black trees all around them. When Eddie slammed his door, a dog started barking inside the Winnebago parked in front of the garage, an old dog from the sound of it, tired and hoarse.

"Quiet, Pudzo," she called out, and immediately the dog shut up.

Pudzo? Eddie thought, following her toward the house. What shit kind of name was that for a dog?

They went inside and got right to it, Eddie cornering her against a wall. Her ass was a bit on the scrawny side maybe, now that he had it in his hands, but she sure could kiss, whoever she was.

"What else do they like to do in Africa?" he asked, coming up for air.

From there they headed over to the couch, then onto the floor, then back onto the couch again, before she waltzed him into her bedroom. He was bare-assed by that time, his bone swinging free, but she still had her jeans on. Any minute now, though, he knew he'd be putting his face where he liked it best. Yeah, he was ready for something like this. Something a little different from the usual fare.

In the bedroom he turned the juice on full, getting her nice and churned up, her eyes shining with a fine animal heat.

"If you don't take those pants off soon," he told her, sprawled across the bed, "I'm gonna rip 'em off."

"Okay, chummy," she said. "You just relax right here, and I'll be back in a second."

Christ, she must be on the rag, Eddie thought, watching her ass work as she went out the door. Well, he didn't mind a little blood if she didn't.

"Bring me a beer," he called after her.

Reaching down, he took hold of himself, absently stroking as he looked around the room. A desk and a matching bureau, white with flowery trim. A round mirror over the desk, framed with photos and strings of pretty beads, and another full-length mirror on the closet door. Two shelves crowded with small ceramic horses and dogs, all neatly arranged in rows. The pale blue walls covered with posters—a sunset, the ocean, a herd of wild giraffes. And on the bed itself, plenty of thick pillows and a bright ruffled quilt with rainbows and stars, plus a whole bunch of soft dolls and stuffed animals piled on the pillows—monkeys and bears, dinosaurs and bunnies.

And me, Eddie thought, giving himself a little teasing squeeze.

Every man had his own personal preferences, of course, but as far as he was concerned, a girl's bedroom, when it looked like this, was about as sexy a place as you could ever hope to find.

Brushing some of the toy animals onto the floor, Eddie grabbed a pillow and made himself comfortable. He could hear what's-her-face in the other room, the bathroom probably, coughing once or twice and clearing her throat. With his free hand he reached out and picked up one of the stuffed toys, a green lizard wearing a little red skirt, a sorry-looking fucker that had obviously seen better days.

"You're in great shape," Eddie muttered, lifting the skirt and exposing the gaping hole between its legs.

Squirming in his hand, the thing suddenly bit into his flesh, clamping down on the web of skin between his thumb and finger. A jolt of pain shot up his arm and Eddie stared at the lizard in disbelief as it squeaked and bit him again, deeper this time, twisting its head from side to side, tearing at the wound.

Panicking, Eddie tried to pull it off, but the thing just wouldn't let go. Writhing angrily, it sank its teeth into his wrist.

"Get the *fuck* off me!" he cried, flailing out and smashing his hand against the headboard, finally knocking it free.

"I see you've begun without me," a voice said behind him.

Startled, Eddie swung around and saw the girl standing naked in the doorway, holding a small black ball in her left hand. She was smiling down at the lizard on the floor, as if waiting for it to respond.

Jesus, Eddie realized. She's talking to it.

"You couldn't wait another minute, right?" She laughed, a slight, tinny sound, hard and humorless.

Between her legs there was a scabby, bloody mess, swollen and raw with infection. Eddie's heart turned to cold stone at the sight.

"Oh well," she said, looking up at him now, her eyes empty and flat. "I hope this hasn't ruined the mood."

Too amazed to say a word, Eddie swung his legs off the opposite side of the bed and slowly stood.

"We can still have fun," the girl said, taking a few steps into the room. Raising her left arm, she held the ball out toward him, a twitchy grin skewing her features. "That's what you want, isn't it? To have some fun?"

Doing what? Eddie thought. Playing fucking catch? No thanks.

He didn't know what the hell was happening here, and he didn't want to know. The party was over and he was going home.

Edging toward the foot of the bed, he kept a wary eye on the girl. He was just wondering where the lizard had gotten to, when it leapt out from under the bed and attached itself to his leg, digging its needle teeth deep into his calf.

Shouting out in pain and shock, Eddie reached down with both hands and tore the screeching thing loose. Staggering forward, he spun and threw it at the

girl's face, pushing past her as she lifted her arms to
ward off the frenzied creature.

He was out the door and already running down the
hall before he realized his mistake. He'd turned the
wrong way. The living room was back in the other
direction. Up ahead there was nothing but two closed
doors and a wall.

Wheeling around, he saw the girl lurching through
the door after him, the lizard right at her heels.

"Stay away from me," he told her. "Just stay the
fuck away."

She cocked her head to one side, like a robin
listening to a worm. Lowering a hand, she fingered
herself for a moment, a thin thread of blood unraveling down her thighs.

"You're a funny guy," she said. "What's the matter?
Don't you like me anymore?"

The hell with this, Eddie decided.

Dropping one shoulder, he bellowed and charged
down the hallway, ready to flatten her if that's what it
took. The next thing he knew, she had him up against
the wall and was stuffing the black ball into his mouth.

Try as he might, he couldn't even begin to break her
hold. Christ, she was strong!

Wild with panic, he jerked his knee up into her
crotch, not once but twice, lifting her clear off the
ground both times. Finally she fell back, but God help
him, she was laughing like crazy now, the lizard
dancing in circles around her feet, chirping excitedly.

"Come on, let's do that some more," she said, still
blocking his way. "I'm getting all tingly inside."

Spinning around, tottering unsteadily, Eddie fled
down the hall. He couldn't understand how it was
possible, but he knew he was no match for her. He

must have outweighed her by at least seventy-five pounds, and yet she'd easily pinned him against that wall.

Opening the first door he came to, he stepped into a large bedroom lit by a single night-table lamp. Slamming the door behind him, he fumbled with the knob for a second before he managed to twist the lock into place. Looking around desperately for a window, he noticed two figures lying motionless on the bed, a man and a woman stretched out flat on their backs, staring up at the ceiling.

A sharp, sinking feeling blossomed in the pit of his stomach. As the door rattled and shook on its hinges, Eddie forced himself to cross the room.

Moving toward the bed, he saw the webby mass of pale blue tendrils sprouting in the woman's mouth, a feathery tangle of tiny pulsing veins that fluttered with every breath she took.

With a splintering crash the door finally broke open behind him.

Weak with dread, his mind as blank as glass, Eddie turned to face the girl. Lifting her arm, she held the ball out toward him once again, and for just an instant Eddie swore he saw the thing quivering in her palm.

"Time to fly," she told him, stepping into the room. "Time to fly."

3

His mouth was a foul pesthole. When she touched him, her skin prickled and contracted. He smelled frankly of sweat and sperm, the rankness of a mature male. He was so pitifully feeble she could've folded him up like a chair, and yet his struggles beneath her sparked a vague heat between her legs. She could feel her pores opening, her inward parts turning soft and slick.

"Let's goo in the muck," she whispered into his ear. "Let's get it wet."

Churning with excitement, longing with a pure fervor, he bucked and thrashed under her, snarling with desire.

A drowning man groping for rescue.

Pure ooze.

"I hope you're a wild one," she added.

Squatting on the edge of her parents' bed, the lizard looked on, its front paws busy beneath the tiny red apron.

A golden-haired lion, Molly thought. That's what she really needed. On her hands and knees in the tall dry grass, with the white sun burning overhead, it would mount her roughly from behind, grunting and then purring as its velvet haunches shuddered against her.

Riding the semiconscious body on the floor, Molly rocked her hips in mechanical urgency, steady and vigorous. Reaching down, she roughly squeezed his scrotal chestnuts, all chubby and pink. Flapping his arms around, he made soft animal love sounds, carried away by his natural enthusiasm.

What's this? Molly thought. A play for sympathy?

Meat had its moments maybe, but it was no solution to boredom.

At the instant of her release, she lifted her eyes to gaze out through the bedroom window, east into the watching night.

CHAPTER SEVEN

~

Hey, hey, hey," Reverend Red Flowers went, gesturing toward the world. "Look there!"

"Ooh, yes," answered Auntie JuJu, giggling girlishly. "A sweet sight, chummy, no? A sweet, sweet sight."

Ignoring their annoying chatter, Sibatia peered westward beyond the bloody waters, far over the moving hills, to the very edge of the last frontier.

The city of dreams was sleeping. The great boulevards were still, the factories and slaughterhouses quiet. The vast stadiums and arenas were empty, the parks and avenues vacant and dark. No American airplanes patrolled the skies, no gunboats plied the labyrinthine canals. The black towers were as silent as tombs, the temple ramparts abandoned. Shadows shrouded every spire and minaret, every obelisk and golden dome.

"Good gosh now," the Reverend said softly. "Would you please just look at her go."

The girl was in the palace near the river, in a corner room on the uppermost floor. Her window was filled with a diffuse amber light. Keeping her eyes locked on

Sibatia's, she thrust herself down on the man underneath her, again and again, her face bright with a pained delight.

Adjusting his grip on the tree, Sibatia gave her a little wave, a small sign of encouragement perhaps. She seemed so distant, so alone.

"Oh, embrace me," Auntie JuJu crooned seductively. "Come and see to my bodily needs."

Bending over, she parted her back legs, teasing the Reverend with her ample beauty. Her crimson skin lay against her bones with no flesh at all beneath it. Across her fair belly, jagged welts and ritual scars rippled invitingly.

Tall and gaunt, wearing only a pair of Michael Jordan wristbands and a necklace of dried testes, Reverend Red Flowers approached her along the limb. His face was all mouth and burning eyes, his bald scarlet skull beaded with black sweat.

"Dear Mother Earth," he mumbled. "It's a gay life here."

Gripping JuJu's supple hourglass waist, he slowly hunkered forward, nipping delicately as he entered her, his filed front teeth leaving prints on her flesh like the tracks of small animals.

Sibatia watched for a moment, then turned back toward the city, only to discover that the palace was now dark, the girl gone.

"Come and join us," JuJu hissed to him. "Chummy, I have plenty of empty holes for you."

"As do I," the Reverend added, puffing like a grumpus as he lustfully pumped away, his joints clacking like knackers, his four balls swinging in the air.

Sibatia was tempted. Why deny it? Though he

wouldn't want to admit it to anyone, the sight of the American girl had aroused him. And truly, rutting with JuJu was always good fun. Already a needle-sharp stream of clear fluid was squirting from her posterior vent as the Reverend briskly caressed the inflamed membranes along her arched spine.

Maybe just a quickie, Sibatia decided, reaching into the pocket of his bag for a prophylactic. Sure, why not?

He was just about to unfasten his trousers when he sensed movement above. A limb shifted, sending a shiver through the dark slick leaves and pale pulpy fruits. For an instant Sibatia caught the sweet smell of rot in the air. There was a whisper of sound like a pail full of hornets rustling in the sun, and then Uncle Dry Skull was there, swinging down from the upper depths to land on a branch directly overhead.

As black as the skeleton of a burnt tree, as black as iron, he stared grimly at JuJu and the Reverend, pointedly unimpressed, his bodeful eyes bright as soap bubbles. Oblivious to his presence, the two lovers continued about their business. When his gaze turned in Sibatia's direction, his jaw snapping open and shut, mouthing the air silently, Sibatia snatched up his seed pouch and immediately started to descend.

He hadn't gone far before the ruckus began above—a warbling cry of surprise followed by a series of muffled grunts and sobs, then an anguished wail as the tree shook and a fine red mist pattered down through the leaves.

Sibatia did not hesitate. He climbed steadily, dropping from limb to limb, the wheezy rhythmic moans overhead soon fading to silence. His arms ached and his breath was a hoarse clatter in his throat, but still he continued on.

Undoubtedly, Dry Skull would be a while with JuJu and the Reverend, but Sibatia was not about to take any chances. The last time Uncle had gotten his hands on him, he had wandered around for days afterward, eating dirt and talking to stones.

Finally, dizzy with fatigue, Sibatia reached the lower levels of the tree. Slowing his pace at last, he allowed himself a brief rest, plucking several fleshy flowers from the nearest limb to quench his thirst. Refreshed, he descended the remainder of the way to the ground, leaping from the bottom branch, his seed pouch clutched tightly to his chest.

Pudzo was there to greet him, along with a small group of waiting villagers, close to a dozen people in all now—the two old Nobambo brothers, a refugee family he had found wandering along the river just hours ago, a pair of orphan girls gathered from the bush, and of course Yolanda, with her son and grandmother.

At his appearance, those who were still able to commenced to murmur and sigh, their naked torsos undulating limply.

Circling the group slowly, Sibatia took a moment to check on how things were progressing. A fine mesh of pinkish tubes and thicker rootlike pipes joined each person securely to his or her neighbor. Fronds of greasy blue filament dangled from every mouth, old and young alike, a lacy fringe that shivered ever so slightly. Except for the odor of shit and clotted blood in the air, Sibatia couldn't have been more pleased.

Coming to a halt before Yolanda, he paused and set down his pouch.

Her face was calm, her eyes closed, her belly swollen now as big as a barrel. A short skirt of nearly transparent tissue hung about her bare waist, a glistening length of veined cable snaking out from beneath it, its ribbed tip buried deep in the chest of the man standing close beside her.

"Okay, everyone," Sibatia said, opening the front of his trousers and stepping into her welcoming embrace. "Group hug, everybody. Come on. Big group hug."

CHAPTER EIGHT

~

1

People lying paralyzed under alien assault, the TV said. An interspecies breeding program has invaded our physical reality.

"Hey, they're on to you." Eddie chuckled, using the remote to adjust the volume. "You've been found out."

A huge range of entities and spirits share our universe, the TV added. I didn't realize I was having sex with aliens until just a few months ago.

We'll be right back . . .

Douche powder and hemorrhoidal cream. Denture cleanser and scented panty shields.

"For Christ's sweet sake," Eddie went, changing the channel. "It doesn't bear thinking about."

Pinching the wound between her fingers, Molly carefully slid the needle into the lizard's crotch, working the thick nylon thread through the rubbery flesh.

"That ain't gonna hold," Eddie told her, sitting beside her on the couch. "No way."

The lizard squirmed on her lap each time Molly pulled the thread taut, staring up at her through shuttered eyes. Purring softly, it rested its delicate little hands on hers.

Let's remember that there are two victims here, the TV said. The young girl, yes, a tragedy, a terrible terrible thing. But I am innocent. I did not commit this crime.

How can you live with yourself?

Excuse me. I did not commit this . . . I did not.

What about the . . . ? Hold on a second. The semen? What about all that semen?

Applause, applause.

"Yeah, what about it?" Eddie asked, jacking the volume still higher. "That's a damn good question."

Forensic evidence? Forensic? Excuse me, may I speak? Forensic evidence? There was none. Excuse me, I'd like a chance to respond to that.

"Who is he fucking trying to kid?" Eddie asked. "He did it, the sick bastard. And he can't wait to do it again. It's all a question of brain chemistry. Color him weird."

Finishing the final few stitches, Molly looped and knotted the thread. Lifting the lizard, she checked her work, trimming the stray ends of nylon with her mother's good sewing scissors.

"You know what?" Eddie said. "I'll bet Geraldo would just love to have you on his show."

Leaning toward him, Molly stabbed the four-inch quilting needle deep into his thigh.

The skin around his mouth shivered for a moment, his dead-white face widening in a dreamy smile. Reaching over, Molly took the remote from him and clicked off the TV.

"Don't tell me," Eddie said. "You hate Geraldo, right? You're an Oprah fan."

Withdrawing the bloody needle from his leg, she rested it against his cheek, pricking the skin just beneath his eye.

"You through yet, dogfuck?" she asked quietly. "You finished making all your funny little jokes?"

Rattled, he paused for a second, motionless and undecided. Finally, he nodded.

"Go wait outside," she told him, handing him the lizard.

Leaving him sitting there, she got to her feet and headed for her parents' bedroom.

When the gods knock, you must answer. When they come for you, you must welcome them with open arms. You must spread your legs and fly. If they happen to fart, then you inhale. What other choice do you have?

None, of course.

True power is always heralded by great pain.

And yet, how could she possibly do this to her parents? No matter the wonders that awaited them, the glories to be revealed.

Standing beside her father's bed, she reached down and took one of his hands in hers. Curled fetally on his side, he gazed unblinkingly past her, toward the window and the daylight outside. Glistening wetly, the blue-black lace stretched his mouth in a snarling yawn.

I can't do it, she realized. Not to my own parents. I just can't.

Moving from window to window, she closed the curtains tight. Taking the small trash basket out from beneath her father's desk, she circled the bed and stood at her mother's side. Grasping the veiny blue mesh between her fingers, she slowly lifted it from her mother's gaping mouth, tugging gently but firmly, snipping several of the fattest filaments with the sewing scissors still in her hand.

A wave of staticky panic swept across her mother's face, then instantly disappeared. Her breath hissed in her throat as she stared up at Molly, her eyes fixed on things deep within.

"Tenapo," she groaned in her dream, as Molly eased the stringy mass from her mouth *"Tenapo suza."*

That's right, Molly thought, hesitating for a moment as the primary root came into sight. That's right, Mom. There's no place to hide.

Inch by inch she worked the seed free, extracting the pale tendrils from her mother's throat. As the slick black sphere finally appeared, Helen raised her hands and clutched weakly at her daughter's arm. She tried to swallow the seed back down, but Molly kept on pulling. Just as her teeth clamped shut, the small dark ball slipped past her lips.

Molly stepped away and took a minute to examine the seed. Except for a puffy nickel-size bruise on its crown, it seemed to be in decent shape. She cut the main tubule at its base, tossing it into the trash can, then trimmed the beard of capillaries hanging from the ball's lower half. Warm beads of spermlike sap soon flecked her hands.

Resting quietly again, her mother lay with her head thrown back, her face pallid and shiny with perspiration, bloody saliva trickling from between her lips.

Taking a deep breath, Molly placed the seed in her own mouth and swallowed.

She never should've chosen her parents. She never

should've come home at all. What had she been thinking of?

What had she been dreaming?

Directing her legs toward the other side of the bed, she felt her stomach clench and begin to swim. She rolled her father onto his back and started right in. She tried to see something in his face besides the pain, but she couldn't. He fought her more than her mother had, gagging and biting at the root as Molly struggled to remove it, his fists striking her feebly on the chest.

Finally, the seed slid out, dangling at the tip of a thin flexible stalk.

"Shit," Molly muttered, immediately spotting the ragged tear along its side. She cut the fringe of stems carefully from the top and bottom, dropping them into the trash basket.

Hoping for the best, Molly placed her father's damaged seed in her mouth and forced it down, the jagged edges tickling her tongue and throat. There was a bitter taste this time that surprised her at first, a spurt of warm fluid seeping from the wound.

She covered her parents with a quilt and slipped a pillow under each of their heads. She stayed with them until they were both sleeping peacefully, her mother snoring softly with every rasping breath.

"Good-bye, Mom. Good-bye, Daddy."

She loved them, she truly did, and her only wish was that they understood she never meant them any harm. Giving them each a kiss on the forehead, she turned away at last and left the room.

She found Harley in the kitchen, sleeping in a patch of sunlight. She filled his bowl to the brim with fresh water and poured half a bag of Gravy Train into a large pot. "See you later, old fella," she said, scratching at his belly for a minute, making one of his back legs dance in the air. "You take good care of them, okay?"

After one final look around the kitchen, she went out through the back door.

Overhead, every cloud in the sky was edged with red, a distant rumble of drums or thunder heralding the approaching storm of blood. From every tree in the yard, vultures sang out in praise of their Lord.

Climbing into the Winnebago, Molly swept the lizard off the driver's seat and threw it into the back. When she glanced over at Eddie, he rolled his eyes around in his sockets, moving one eyelid as if in a wink.

"Quit that," she told him, and with a bored shrug he turned away.

The RV chugged and huffed, and then fired right up. Putting it in gear, Molly backed out of the driveway.

When all this is over with, she promised herself, *I'll return here. In the warm red rain, I'll return to my home.*

"Chummy, you're never going to see this place again," Eddie went, checking his side of the road for oncoming traffic. "Not even in your dreams."

2

The moment the nose of the van crossed the border into Vermont, Aileen lit up some of the Mexican weed. Ben slid a Dead tape in and hunched forward over the wheel, the van zooming along now with easy speed. As Garcia warbled, Aileen passed the joint Ben's way.

"Everybody sees things from their own angle," she said, the words rolling from her mouth in a pall of smoke. "And all these angles are the archetypes of the things you need to know to cover your ass."

"From their own angel?" Ben asked.

"Angle," Aileen told him. *"Angle."*

Maybe so, Ben thought, helping himself to a headful of Mexico. Maybe so.

Personally, though, he was getting mighty tired of her gassing about everything. To his way of thinking, you had to transcend your particular hang-ups and just go on instinct. Plain and simple.

"It's totally amorphous," he told her.

"Ben, you're an A-list guy." She reached over for the joint, swiping it deftly from between his fingers. "But no approval can win you like your own respect."

"I've heard that."

"So quit being such a weenie," she added. "Or you'll spook things up, royally."

Sad as it might sound, if she wasn't such a primo little fuck, he'd give serious consideration to dumping her. He wasn't programmed for something like her, and hopefully never would be. Sure, you could look at her as a gnarly learning experience, but lately he'd been getting into some chaotic spaces with her, skanky spaces he hadn't seen in quite a while.

"How about if we stop in Brattleboro for breakfast?" he suggested. "We could grab a bagel and some java."

"Man, let's just keep going, okay?"

Things being what they were, that was probably the better idea. It was another two hours yet to the Farm. Last night in Boston had been a crusher, a damn fine party to be sure. There was no school to go to for some of the splendid shit that happened in that city. But he was paying the price now, big-time.

Wafted by the fumes, Ben essayed a smile and steered the van northward into the morning. Brattleboro came and went, the highway climbing slowly now into the hills, mile after easy mile. Aileen dozed off for a bit, slipping over into the land of pure gravy. But when Ben went to notch the Dead up a tad, she bolted right up again, grabbed the tape and chucked it out the window.

"How come we always listen to this tired bullshit? It's fucking older than I am."

Ben's flash was to reach over there and rap his knuckles on the corner of her head. But hey, he was an easygoing soul, right? No need to get ornery. Just hang on and see how it all pans out.

Anyway, it was her tape. And this was her van. And her dope.

"Maybe for a change of pace you could try stepping on the gas a little," she told him, her face twisting with exasperation, her dark eyes driving straight into his. "Christ, we're going about ten miles an hour."

Not so, Ben saw, scrutinizing the dials. They were cruising at a steady fifty, same as—*whoa!*

What's this?

The oil light was flashing red. On, off, then on again—so bright it was like the rest of the world had suddenly turned black-and-white.

Off. On. Off. Then on for good, Ben going, "What a piece of luck," tapping at the dash with his finger, Aileen leaning over to take a closer look.

"What's that light mean?" she asked suspiciously.

"It means something's not right," Ben said, checking the mirrors, as if maybe there might just happen to be a tow truck following along behind them. "It looks like an oil kind of a problem. We should probably pull over."

"Unreal."

Ben kept on driving, though, trying to keep his center, hoping for the best. He just couldn't see this happening.

"So, pull over," Aileen finally went. "Maybe it's only tired, or something."

Ben let her coast, easing onto the shoulder. Just as they rolled to a halt, a black Corvette roared by, horn wailing derisively, a burly arm jabbing out the window to give them the finger.

"I don't think I want to deal with this," Aileen said as Ben turned off the ignition. "This is classic."

Yes sir, Ben thought, climbing out of the van. We're hitting some nice spaces here. Very nice indeed.

Once he managed to find it, the oil stick read perfect, right up level with the Full. Ben stared at the engine for a while, checking for dangling wires, broken belts, or maybe some stray sea gulls sucked into the intake vents.

"Pretty bizarre," he muttered. "Everything looks okay to me."

"I'm taking a piss," Aileen said wearily, walking off into the roadside grass.

Scratching at his beard, Ben did a slow three-sixty. Green hills, blue sky, no clouds, a highway. Where the hell exactly were they, anyway? They'd passed the two Brattleboro exits, what—maybe twenty minutes ago? Any other exits since then?

"Say," he called over to Aileen. "Did we go by Bellows Falls yet?"

He wasn't positive, but he tended to doubt he'd ever been scowled at before by somebody as they squatted to pee.

"You're blind as a melon, you know that, Ben? Bellows Falls? Yeah, we passed it."

When he got behind the wheel again and tried turning the motor over, it started right away. The red light stayed off and the engine didn't make any peculiar noises to speak of. He let it idle for a minute, then pushed the accelerator down and watched the red bulb.

Nothing.

"So?" Aileen asked, climbing in. "What's happening now?"

Ben shrugged and put the van in gear. "Heigh-ho," he said, driving away.

He had it up to third and was just beginning to rethink the whole situation when something started clattering in the back, the engine knocking like it had just taken a direct hit of flak. The van bucked and instantly died, and Ben guided it in for a safe landing on the shoulder of the road.

"Well, we're fucked now," Aileen said, leaning back in her seat and shutting her eyes.

Unequivocally, Ben thought. "How about another joint?"

3

Leaping from the grass, the hyena might've made it if it hadn't hesitated for just an instant on the shoulder. Molly swerved to avoid it, but the arching body hit the grill with a solid thud, passing under the RV's right front wheel. Looking through the sideview mirror, she saw the splayed form skidding back along the road, tumbling in slow motion.

"Cows are worth two points," Eddie remarked idly. "And hitchhikers are good for five."

Molly selected a wafer from the open tin sitting on the console between the seats. "Help yourself," she told Eddie.

He grabbed one and snapped it in half, giving the smaller piece to the lizard. "This little shit have a name?" he asked.

Riding up on the dash, the lizard nibbled at the cracker, enjoying the view through the windshield.

"Yeah. Eddie Junior."

"Well, hell. Come to think of it, he kind of looks like me, doesn't he?"

"Listen," Molly said, "from now on, if you feel the need to make noise, just use your asshole, okay? I'm tired of hearing your mouth."

"Sure," Eddie answered, his face coming around slow and tight. "Say, are we almost there yet?"

Narrow gorges and ravines opened on either side of the interstate, the highland foothills thick with acacias, umbrella thorns, and soaring fever trees as brilliant as October maples, yellow and orange shot with shimmering gold. Fenced pastures and farmland, gray barns and neat white houses. Ghostly fields of corn and wide meadows dense with flowers and mist. In the near distance, soft hills with scattered outcrops of boulders rose beyond a bright silver-blue stretch of the Connecticut River.

She could see things clearly now, see them as they were meant to be seen.

North to Canada, then west to the Rockies—maybe she should just keep on driving this thing straight through to California, out to redwood country where the trees were as old as stone. She could feel the road humming in her hands as she gripped the wheel.

"Bellows-fucking-Falls," Eddie muttered as they dipped down into a valley and the town was suddenly right there, spread out beneath the shadow of Breakneck Mountain, the streets lined with brick storefronts and old churches, a grid of well-tended houses and a shopping center or two, a cemetery and a baseball diamond, a factory, a lumberyard, and the regional high school.

Office buildings and parking lots, monuments and parks, all scratched out and molded by the planet's filthiest and cruelest animal. No matter how remote or faraway, there was no place left on Earth that remained completely untouched by his kind. Even the moon had been fouled, feces dumped beneath the stars, craters filled with spare parts and trash.

Time to thin the herd, Molly thought.

On the outskirts of town a neighborhood of

thatched beehive huts was burning, soldiers rounding up the women and children into trucks. From the belly of a helicopter hovering overhead, a half-dozen ropes hung down, a naked man dangling from each one, dancing in the air just above the highest flames.

The sound of a nearby horn snapped Molly's attention back to the road. A tan Safari cruised by in the fast lane, a fellow RVer bound for sunnier climes. Behind the tinted windows of the living quarters, a pair of kids were bouncing up and down, their toy rifles pointed straight at Molly. Snatching the lizard off the dashboard, she thrust it out her window, stretching her arm so that the flailing creature was right in front of the kids' astonished faces, both of them abruptly ducking from sight as the Safari sped away.

"Goofy highjinks," Eddie said as Molly reeled the lizard in and replaced it on the dash. "Big, big fun."

4

Seeds from outer space," Ben declared, watching the milkweeds fly from Aileen's hand. "Extraterrestrial spores."

Aileen waved her arm again, sending another batch of silky parachutes drifting across the highway. "I hate to tell you this, Captain, but we're still on Terra. We beamed up, all right, but we're still here."

"No, seriously." Ben sat down on the van's rear bumper. When Aileen offered him what was left of the second joint, he took a quick hit and handed it right back. The sun was smack in his eyes, mixing with the steady whir of the insects singing in the grass. Settling into the day, Ben was feeling a certain loony mellowness. "I was talking to this guy last night at the party. The guy with all the coke?"

"And the drum?"

"The gun?"

"Drum."

"No, I mean the other guy with all the coke. The one whose girlfriend only had one hand."

"Oh, yeah."

A pack of cars suddenly slipped by, all doing close to eighty. Ben stuck his thumb out without bothering to stand.

"Which reminds me. Her hand? The missing one? I swear it wasn't the same one the whole time."

"Sure, Ben. Whatever."

"In all seriousness. Right at the end there, right before they left? I'm not kidding, it was like she switched her hands around or something. I remember noticing it."

Traffic was picking up. A BMW slowed to take a look at Aileen, then zipped away when the driver spotted Ben sitting there. Aileen killed the joint and flicked the roach into the road.

"The thing with the seeds, though," Ben went on. "From what this guy was telling me, it's one of those things, you know, where even if it's not true, it ought to be."

Aileen tore another pod off the milkweed plant and broke it open. The tiny white puffs scattered against the sky as Ben took a moment to collect his thoughts.

"What it comes down to, basically, is that there's all

this outrageous stuff floating around in space, okay? All sorts of molecules and micro-organisms and shit. Maybe only one iota of it every million square miles, or whatever, but it's definitely out there."

"Where'd it come from?" Aileen asked.

"Who knows? Planets blasted to pieces when their suns went nova, maybe. Or here's the real kicker— maybe the stuff's deliberately being spread around."

"Yeah? By who?"

Aileen tried her luck hitchhiking to a passing RV, but the thing roared by in a gust of wind. "Thanks a lot!" she called after it. *"Jerkoff!"*

"Like I said, who knows?" Ben continued. "But according to this guy, certain spores will last just about forever if you keep them in a total vacuum, you know, like way out in deep space?"

"So?"

"So, just listen. Suppose back when the Earth was just getting started, we happened to cruise through some of this stuff. Suppose spores designed by an alien intelligence seeded the Earth, or fertilized it, and everything since then is the result of that. And what if like tomorrow something else decides to come along, somebody else's bullshit? Damn near anything could be floating around out there, right? Bacteria, viruses, all that. I mean, how would we even know, until we hit it?"

"Beats me."

"And if it happened here, it sure as hell could happen other places too. There may or may not be Earths all over the goddamn place. It's like we're aliens, you know? Like this is not really our true home world."

"Invasion of the Body Snatchers," Aileen said.

"Didn't those pod-things originally come from outer space somewhere?"

But Ben wasn't listening. He was thinking cancer. He was thinking AIDS. He was thinking, Whoa, what next?

And then another RV came tooling down the road.

5

As the two ass scratchers climbed in, Molly watched a pack of hyenas gathered around a fallen zebra in the grass, ripping at its open belly.

"Where you folks headed?" Eddie asked cheerfully. "Where's your tribe at?"

The guy seemed to be having some trouble with the side door, but then he finally figured out how to get it shut. One by one the hyenas raised their bloody snouts from their meal to peer toward the road, a string of vultures waiting patiently behind them. Molly put the Winnebago in gear and drove off, the lizard hiding on the floor between her legs, its BB eyes bright with anticipation.

"Next exit, I guess," the field hippie said, kneeling on the carpet beside the girl. "Van's broken down. We need to find a gas station, or maybe a phone. My name's Ben," he added, shaking hands with Eddie and nodding hello to Molly. "And this is Aileen."

"Hi," Aileen went. "Pretty neat wheels you have here. Lots of space. Where you taking it?"

"Hell if I know," Eddie confided. "I'm just along for the ride."

Ben grinned. "That's cool."

"Here, have a cracker," Molly said, offering the tin.

"Ah, breakfast." Ben took two and handed one to the girl.

Keeping an eye on the road, Molly watched them suck the wafers into their faces. The air was thick with their scent, smoke and patchouli oil on top of ripe sweat. A spidery shiver ascended her spine, and she felt a sudden cherry-red urge to end it all, to send the RV careening into the next bridge abutment. The thought of what needed to be done here, with these two straggly dreadheads, was almost too much to bear.

But there wasn't time to waver again. In the darkness behind her eyes she could feel a presence gathering. She must not forget her Lord in the difficult work of approaching Him. From the roots of her being, her prayers must rise from her heart like the finest of flowers on the World Tree, radiant with a fruitful joyousness.

"Got any dope?" Eddie asked congenially.

"Um, not really," Ben replied. "But listen, that reminds me," he said, turning to his partner. "Sacred mushrooms, okay? Psilocybin? Peyote? There's no way that stuff evolved here on Earth. There's nothing else remotely like it around. They've run all kinds of tests—out in California, I think it was—and it turns out mushroom spores can easily survive in deep space. Food of the gods, man, I'm telling you. Food of the fucking gods."

"Don't you just love these guys?" Eddie said quietly, leaning toward Molly and shaking his head. "Crazy as catshit, if you ask me."

Outside the windshield, the landscape spread away

in a haze of golden grass, great lion-colored fields, silent and still. Treeless hills rose in the distance, the dark mountains beyond holding back the sky.

"You wouldn't happen to have a spare cigarette, would you?" Ben asked.

Molly handed him the half-empty pack of her father's lying on the dashboard. "Keep 'em," she said.

"Thanks." He bared his crooked teeth at her, his bloodshot eyes as blue as blue glass.

"Hey, Stuff," Eddie said, addressing Aileen, guiding the conversation in a different direction. "You fuck around much?"

Molly felt the lizard stirring at her feet. She gave Eddie a look, but he ignored her.

"What's that supposed to mean?" Aileen asked.

"Well, hey, like, you know," said Eddie. "There's a bed right in the back there, and I just thought, if you wanted to fuck around some, maybe you and me could—"

"I don't think so," Ben spoke up, getting off his knees to crouch on the balls of his feet. "Man, what a bogus thing to say."

"Hey, sorry." Eddie shrugged and scratched his head, as if taken aback by Ben's reaction. "I saw the big tits, and that Earth mother getup she's wearing, and I just figured she might like some dick. So sue me, I was wrong."

"What's the story with him?" Aileen asked Molly. "Does he have some kind of mental problem, or what?"

"Take it easy, you scruffty freak," Eddie went. "Don't get your neck all in a knot. By the way, you don't have anything contagious, do you?"

131

"Fuck you," Ben said.

"Come on now, Mister Natural," Eddie told him. "No need to get excited. Just go with the flow, eh *compadre?* Try a little Zen, or something. Seems to me your yin-yang might be out of whack. Oh, Christ."

And with that he suddenly leaned forward and puked up a dense white jam, a lumpy sweet-smelling pudding that splashed onto the carpet between the seats.

Molly immediately pulled the RV onto the shoulder of the highway as Ben and Aileen cursed and moved back. Gagging loudly, Eddie vomited out another mouthful, a pale pasty pap woven with spaghetti-thin strands of blue tissue.

Braking, Molly brought the Winnebago to a hurried halt. Eddie groaned and sagged against his door, a wormy noodle dangling from one corner of his mouth.

"Your friend doesn't look so hot," Aileen said with disgust, bringing a shaky hand up to her face.

"Yeah," Ben agreed. "Maybe something's out of fuckin' whack."

Clutching the wheel, Molly closed her eyes and drew a deep breath. The limbs of the World Tree, she reminded herself, pierce every last soul.

Carefully climbing over the mess on the floor, she kicked Ben square in the belly. Grasping Aileen by her long hair, she swung her head forward and down against the corner of the dinette table, the force of the blow sending a tremor through the entire RV.

Huffing for air, Ben rolled onto his side, his arms wrapped around his midsection. Molly kicked him again, this time right below the ribs, as the lizard hopped onto his chest and began tearing at his face. Swatting it away, Molly dragged Aileen over to the john and shoved her inside, closing the metal door behind her.

"Oh, man . . ." Ben moaned, struggling slowly onto one knee. When he saw the lizard cavorting at Molly's side, he whimpered like a baby in pain. "What the *hell* is going on?"

Find joy in the doing, Molly thought. With a deep hitching shudder, she brought up a seed, her throat burning as she choked and spat it out.

"Don't worry, Mister Natural," Eddie said, stepping unsteadily between the seats. "This happy horseshit here, it's all in your head."

6

A small wind shivered the trees. Dusk was filling the hills with shadows.

Arthur scanned the ground carefully, as if looking for sign. Charlie waited, watching his son-in-law, cradling his gun in his arms.

"Okay," Arthur said at last, gesturing with the barrel of his rifle toward a thicket of pine. "Over this way."

His T-shirt was stained and sweaty, and his belly hung over his lowslung jeans. He had a twitch that kept jumping on the left side of his face. A fat white fly landed on the back of his arm and he gave it a hard slap, but the thing was so tough and springy it simply flew off.

"Right over here, Charlie," he said again. "I'll show you."

They climbed a slight rise, passing through the

trees, Charlie pausing for a moment to catch his breath. His throat was dry and raw, and his stomach was giving him some trouble.

Arthur glanced back, smiling in a vague, sleepy way. "You gonna make it, Charlie?"

As they neared the top of the hill, the trees thinned, giving way to thick underbrush and scrub. Between the dark crowns of the tallest pines, Charlie saw the silver moon riding in a blue-gray sky.

There was a sudden flash of red off to the right, and Arthur snapped his rifle to his shoulder. Something rattled in the leaves.

Charlie clicked his safety off, his heart racing in his throat and ears.

"Gone," Arthur said, lowering his gun. "He's a sneaky son of a bitch, I'll give him that."

They continued walking. The very top of the hill was bare, with a single odd-looking tree standing in the center of a patch of grass.

"Right over here, Charlie," Arthur told him, stepping aside so that Charlie could go by.

Making his way toward the tree, Charlie brushed at the slow pale flies clinging to his arms. Black husks like Styrofoam peanuts were scattered everywhere on the ground, empty little corpses popping beneath his feet.

The tree was short and squat, its dark gnarled branches twisted spastically above the contorted trunk. As Charlie approached, he noticed a fretful quivering in the limbs, a rhythmic, riffling pulse. The bark was slick and smooth, greasy in the fading light.

"Go ahead," Arthur said behind him.

Keeping his distance, Charlie circled the tree. He

134

thought he heard a rustling murmur, like someone whispering . . .

"Over here, you fuck," it hissed.

He saw the black face on the trunk at the exact instant the face turned and saw him.

It was made of the same dark material as the bark, a living human mask, a face just sitting there, growing on the tree. A polished brow, a yawning jaw, eyes sparkling as the lips pulled back in a gleeful feral leer.

"Cometh ye and taste of my fruit, you sorry sac of piss," it said. "Come give your buddy Sib a little suck."

As the gelled eyes widened and glanced downward, Charlie noticed the cock and balls jutting from the tree, stirring to life as he stared.

"Check this out," Arthur said jocularly, grinning with real joy. Edging warily forward, he touched the heavy penis with the tip of his rifle, stroking it lightly.

"What? You want some more?" the face asked. "You're a tough guy, huh? You a tough guy? Shit. Why don't you get a job, ass-wipe?"

The dark cock hardened and soon stood erect. Arthur laughed softly to himself and kept working at it with his gun, teasing and tickling.

"Better move on back," he eventually said to Charlie. "Old knothead here is just chock-full of seed."

The face was panting now, making strange fartlike sounds in its throat, its eyes fixed on Charlie.

"Time to wake up," it grunted. "Time to wake up, *Daddy.*"

"Oopsy-daisy," said Arthur.

And then the cock spasmed, spurting out a stream of white flies, myriad milky specks buzzing in the air, all swarming straight toward Charlie as the tree shook and the face grimaced wildly and began to howl and yap . . . until, with a sharp cry, Charlie awoke, lying in his bed.

His heart lurched and his body suddenly felt hollow. Something had a hold on him and wouldn't let go.

When he tried to lift his head, a barbed pain erupted behind his eyes and he could hear the screaming tree again, the sticky pale flies clinging to his face and arms. There was a dark vomitlike taste in his mouth, and his vision kept going blurry.

Rolling onto his back, gasping for air, he felt someone close beside him. When he turned, Helen was lying right there.

Her eyes were open and cast back in her head. A fine froth of saliva outlined her lips. Her chest rose and fell laboriously, her breath whistling weakly in her throat.

"Helen?" When he touched her cheek, her skin felt feverish. "Helen?"

Finally, her eyelids fluttered and she let out a soft moan. "Molly," she said in a whispery voice.

She opened and closed her mouth several times, but didn't say anything more. Charlie reached for her, holding her as best as he could. She went limp after a few moments, and he lowered her onto the pillow. He smoothed the damp hair at her temples and wiped the spit from around her lips.

Molly . . .

Oh, Jesus.

It all came rushing back at once. How she had gone insane out at Sherman's Pond, attacking him and shoving that black ball into his mouth. How he'd

136

fought her off, but not for long, helpless against her strength.

And then—nothing.

Nothing but a sick, sick nightmare—*Over here, you fuck!*—and the memory of that black ball, sliding down his throat . . .

Very slowly, Charlie eased his arms out from around Helen and sat up. She seemed to be sleeping peacefully now, although her breathing was still ragged and shallow.

How long had they been lying in bed like this? What in God's name had Molly *done* to them?

Fighting a fresh surge of nausea, Charlie pulled back the blanket and swung his legs off the bed. Feeling light and papery, a sudden fleeting dizziness assailed him, the room whirling for a second or two, woozy and weightless.

Taking short uneasy steps, he crossed the room and headed out the door, bracing one hand against the wall for support. Wagging his tail happily, Harley met him in the hallway.

Molly's bedroom was empty, her bed neatly made. In the living room, Charlie found a pair of men's underwear lying beside the couch. When he saw the clock on the mantel, an ugly chill shot through his bones.

Eleven-thirty.

He'd been unconscious for close to two hours.

In the kitchen, at the tap, he drank long and breathlessly, resting his elbows on the cold edge of the sink. He wet his hands and rubbed his face, trying to ignore the queasy roiling deep in his gut.

Standing at the back door, Harley started whining

again, asking to be let out. Shuffling over to open the screen, Charlie saw that the RV was gone, and that an old green Chevy was parked in the driveway behind his car.

And then he noticed something else as well.

On the small key-shaped board hanging right next to the door, the keys to the cabin were missing.

CHAPTER NINE

A sloughy, sucking sound. A ghost sound, just at the limits of hearing. He could feel it beneath his skin.

Red fissures opening and closing with cryptic intent, her stubby oddities and blunt knobs thrusting in phallic rhythm. Flush with nectar, her umbilicals fluttered teasingly, motioning him nearer. Gnarled bulblike nodules set in chunks of flesh seeped a thick yellow mucilage, sweet with the smell of decomposition and decay, the heady odor of transformation.

The scent of angels . . .

Sibatia closed his eyes and breathed in the jaunty stench of her. She really was a beauty.

A gift from above.

No matter where you grabbed her, you more than got your hands full. It did his heart good just to look at her.

The baby-blue lesions and ballooning pox. The crimson fibroid tassels undulating softly, bumping incessantly against one another, stirred by an invisible tide. The bulky black seed caches, the electric-green data sacs, the accretion disks and globules of plasm.

It came to him that he could accomplish great things here. In fact, there was no end to what he might do.

Keenau Sibatia, cyber-shaman.

Bush wizard.

He would see to America first, but after that, who knows? Perhaps he would take a bit of a vacation and visit the Grandfathers, shining like gold against the blackness of space.

Why not?

When Sibatia was a young boy, his mother had often told him the story of her own visit to a Grandfather.

"We climbed into his damn fool mouth," she would always say toward the end of the tale, shaking her head in genuine disbelief. "He nodded off, and we climbed right in, just to find out what it was like."

Sibatia wished he could've seen her, standing inside that dreaming Grandfather's mouth, her arms outspread for balance, peering down into the Old One's throat.

It was something Sibatia wanted to try someday.

Of course, poking around inside a Grandmother would be even better, but that was one adventure that was going to have to wait a while. At least until he worked the kinks out of this Angel.

"Hey, dog," he said as Pudzo wandered out of the trees, sauntering over to the hut-sized mound to sniff and lift his back leg. "Get the hell away from that."

Morphing and melding, the Angel certainly was growing at a remarkable rate. True, there were a few wavery, soggy sections. But for the most part she was hard-packed and taut, a garden of fruiting corpse meat, prehensile sprigs and nubbles festooning her sun-spackled flanks.

Briefly, Sibatia wondered how everything was shaping up on the inside, where the real magic came to play. What carefree nightmares were forming within her young heart?

Circling her slowly, he came upon the boy's face around back, halfway up the assemblage, surrounded by a patch of red-and-white gangling papillae. Sibatia stood and considered for a few moments, recalling the boy and his mother, Yolanda, her struggles during the first stages of absorption, her sweet swollen belly and gentle cries for mercy.

Stiff and gray, from his high perch the boy stared down at Sibatia now, eyes as glassy as ice, his lips moving rapidly but without making a sound. Seeing the blood-grimed creeper plugged into his skull, Sibatia stepped closer and gave the face a hard slap. The boy's tongue poked out and his eyes rolled up, the muscles along his jaw jumping reflexively.

"Come on out, you old shit," Sibatia said, giving the boy a second slap. "I know it's you."

An expression of fear flashed across the boy's features, blue froth bubbling around the edge of his lips.

"Ah, Sibatia," he finally said in a spacey whisper, speaking with Meru's voice. "I have been waiting."

Sibatia let out a loud contemptuous laugh. Hearing the boy, Pudzo started snarling, Sibatia silencing him with a kick.

"Don't you have anything better to do, old-timer?" he asked, leaning forward until his face was just inches from the boy's. "What's the problem? Jesus kick you out of His bed?"

"I have been wait—" The vine feeding into his skull twitched erratically. "Yes. Yes . . . Such undertakings might diminish mounting strains and temporal gaps . . . Tour leaders have been carefully trained. We don't take a trip, the trip takes us."

Shit, Sibatia thought. No fool like an old fool.

"Tidy up those thoughts, *mganga*," he told the boy. "Don't go all wonky on me now, you nutless fuck."

"Death," Meru said after a moment. "It changes a man."

Sibatia laughed again. "Hey, I've been there. Tell me something I don't know."

"The world's gotten bigger, or I've gotten smaller," Meru went, ignoring Sibatia, focusing his attention inward. "My mind feels strong, though. I've seen so many things."

"You ain't seen squat," Sibatia told him. "You never have, and you sure as hell aren't about to now."

The boy's face was calm with a dreamy repose. "You know, it's not a very good idea to kill someone more powerful than yourself."

"Is that right?" Sibatia replied.

"And another thing," Meru said. "Never get out of the boat unless you're going all the way."

"Is that the best you can do?" Sibatia asked the boy. "Why don't you just give it up? Go wash your feet in the River Jordan. Go stay dead, and quit bothering me."

The Angel shifted then, and the boy grinned.

"Remember, Sibatia. Of all the things that can happen to a dreamer, awakening is always the one he least expects."

Well, enough of this bullshit, Sibatia decided.

"So long, old man," he said. "Show's over."

Reaching out, he clamped one hand against the boy's mouth, pinching his nostrils tightly shut with the other hand. The face mewled and wiggled, trying desperately to bite him. Sibatia shuddered involuntarily, and Pudzo started to bark.

Finally, Sibatia snatched at the tube socketed into the top of the boy's skull. Ripping it free, he stepped back and watched the light drain from the boy's jiggling eyes.

Say good night, Father.

Sweet dreams.

CHAPTER TEN

1

Eddie Starling was in the rear of the RV, keeping an eye on the freaks. Things had been a little hectic for a while there, but mellow was the operative word now. These scraggly nutbars were both way over the top, no doubt drifting in a deep alpha state. Fried, the pair of them.

Stretched out on the rug, Mister Natural was as lively as a log. The only part of that hairy body of his that was moving was his eyes, winking and twitching, bulging and jumping, first one and then the other, but never both together. The dubious fucker, what the hell was he seeing inside that empty head of his?

Meanwhile, over on the bed, his soulmate was breathing like a wounded animal, staring up at the ceiling, lost in happy thoughts. Every minute or so she'd give a chuckle and wave her hands around, moving her feet up and down—left, right, left, right —like maybe she was climbing the stairway to heaven.

The more Eddie watched her, the tastier she looked. A bit stout, okay, but she sure gave his cock a throb.

Time for some touchy-feely? Eddie let himself be persuaded. Shit, why not?

Scooching on over there, the world outside the windows zooming by at warp speed, Eddie sat down on the edge of the bed. "Hello, Stuff," he said, sliding his hand under her blouse.

Bingo—no bra. And what's this? Well into the spirit of things, her nipples were already standing at attention, plucky little devils, nuzzling comfortably against his palm.

Bending down, Eddie licked the bloody egg rising from her forehead, where she'd hit the table. "No thrills without chills, right, Stuff?"

He gave her teat a pinch, and when she didn't respond, he gave her another. Rocking little angel, let me kiss my blues away.

"Okay, Studly," Molly called from the front of the RV. "That's about enough."

Could that possibly be a note of jealousy he detected in her voice?

"I'm not sure I understand what the problem is," he told her.

"Let it heal," she said. "Just leave her alone."

Oh yeah. Let it heal. Of course.

Giving her a final tweak, Eddie removed his hand and straightened the girl's blouse. Despite all the hard miles on her face, and the stench of incense and dope wafting off her raggedy clothes, and the wild hair everywhere, she really was quite a cutie.

"Later," he said, patting her belly as her feet started in again—left, right, left—the RV slowing now and easing off the highway, coasting down the exit ramp to Heebiejeebieville, Eddie figured. At last.

Through the bug-splattered windows there wasn't

all that much to see. Fields of tall green corn and an occasional dirty white farmhouse or trailer, every front yard cluttered with a Sunday-morning tag sale. A cemetery, a John Deere dealership, a bunch of cows standing around sniffing each other's rear ends. Cruising along, Molly put a cassette in the tape deck, Mr. Frank Sinatra, singing about how there wouldn't be no sorrow, tomorrow.

Ol' Dead Eyes.

And just like that, the RV was suddenly stopped, and Molly was opening her door and climbing out from behind the wheel.

What'd I miss? Eddie wondered, snapping back to the big here and now. Jeez, you hang around with these freaking hairfaces, and the next thing you know you're doing hippie fade-outs.

Leaning forward, Eddie peered out the window. A Quick-Check-Jiffy-Shoppe sort of a place, with a gas pump out front. Bud Lite and two-percent milk only $1.98 a gallon. Megabucks and live bait.

Hey, was he or was he not on vacation here? So how about a six-pack? Fuck knows, he could use a couple cold ones.

"You guys in the mood for some brews?" he asked. "Yo, Mister Natural. Two blinks means yes. All right, bro. Relax. Down, boy. I'll get us a case."

Sure thing. And once we get to wherever it is we're going, we'll have ourselves a damn crack little party.

Outside on the driver's side of the RV, Molly was filling the tank with gas. Keeping a low profile, Eddie went over to the back door on the opposite side and eased it open. The moment he did, the lizard skulked into sight between the front seats, hissing softly as it scuttered forward on all fours.

146

"Don't you come near me, you fucking newt," Eddie told it. "I swear I'll do an Ozzy Osbourne with your head."

The lizard hesitated, and Eddie slipped out the door, clicking it quietly shut behind him.

Screened from Molly by the Winnebago, he walked across the lot toward the store. Up and moving around, his brain box was a bit jangly maybe, but otherwise it was all systems go. His body felt simple and strong. He liked the way his muscles and such tugged against his bones, every last organ inside him doing its job.

The parking lot was empty, with nary a tourist in sight. When he entered the store, there was no one inside but the girl behind the counter.

"Hiya," he said as she glanced his way. "How's it going?"

Firmly fleshed, a big-girl body full of juice, so fresh and clean she sparkled. A hormone honey with shaggy dark hair. Seventeen, eighteen tops. Yes sir, live bait.

"Morning," she replied, showing him some teeth.

She wants me, Eddie thought, heading for the coolers in the rear of the store. Her little pet mouse is already panting.

Pork and beans, licorice whips, Kotex and a rack of Stephen King books. The aisles were all hard lines and bright light. Porno magazines and mayonnaise.

Eddie grabbed four six-packs from behind the glass doors, picking different brands at random, the cost be damned, figuring that his new pals would be partial to at least one.

As he approached the register, the girl turned her back toward him and made as if to adjust some merchandise on a low shelf. He checked out her ass as

she intended him to, and found it to be quite inviting
indeed.

Oh, misery me.

"All set?" she asked, giving her hair a flounce.

Eddie lined up the beer on the counter. KIM said the
perky name tag on her chest. Hot black eyes and a
friendly Kimmy-smile. A pretty red blouse the same
Kimmy-color as her nails. His blood quickened as her
gaze drifted south, sizing him up, lingering for a
moment on the puke stains in his lap.

She's yours for the taking, Eddie told himself. You
can open her up and climb right the fuck inside her, if
you want.

"This everything?" she went.

Well now, I guess not, Eddie decided.

Reaching into his pocket for his wallet, he took out
a rubber from his stash, going with a black ribbed
number, always a popular choice with the ladies.
From the display rack on top of the deli case, he
selected a ten-inch Spring Tree pepperoni. Using his
teeth to open the package, he unwrapped the cylinder
of meat.

"What are you doing?" Kim said, sounding a bit
sniffy now, stepping away from the register as Eddie
deftly slipped the condom onto the tip of the pepperoni. "What the hell are you doing?"

Eddie gave her a little laugh, trying to keep things
light.

"No offense, Kim," he said, sliding the rubber the
rest of the way on. "But these days, it just doesn't
make sense to take chances."

A mask of bewilderment closed over her features.
Her face blanched and she took another step back,

then one to the side, a little dance of confusion and fear. A mating dance, perhaps.

Watching her eyes, Eddie felt a tender aching deep within him. "My flesh quivers at your call," he told her.

She made a move to step out from behind the counter, but he blocked her way. "I'll give you the money," she said. "All of it."

"That's okay, Kim. The first time's free." He slid the pepperoni into his mouth for a moment, slicking it up. "Such things add romance to a life, wouldn't you say?"

She bolted then, and he knocked her the hell down. When he climbed onto her, she bucked and twisted and tried to bite his arm. Man, what's with the attitude? he wondered. Some kind of female thing?

When she started calling out for help, he used his fist against her skull.

Some fun, huh?

"Does this make pictures in your head?" he asked, punching her again.

He still had the fucking touch. Before long she was making appreciative noises, and then she turned on the waterworks and pissed herself.

All right, enough foreplay.

Forcing her legs apart, he pushed her little Kimmy-skirt up around her waist and got to work, like the iron man he was, him boning and her moaning, his balls clanging away, big with seed. There was still plenty of giddy-up left in her, though, and she began fighting him once more, her blue eyes fired with pain.

He was just about to give her a taste of pepperoni, when he heard the door open, and then suddenly there was Molly, leaning over the counter, with a definite look of disappointment on her face.

2

On wobbly legs, nauseous and disoriented, Charlie returned to the bedroom. He tried to rouse Helen again, but she just wouldn't wake up. She still seemed awfully warm to the touch, and her breathing was shallower than ever. When he checked her pulse, he thought it felt stronger, although his own heart was racing so hard he couldn't be sure.

Leaning back against the headboard, he closed his eyes for a moment, trying to decide what he should do. Call the police? Call Rescue? What?

Suddenly Helen sat bolt upright, scaring him half to death.

"Charlie, we have to go after her," she announced evenly. "She's on her way to the cabin."

Too astonished to react otherwise, Charlie simply stared at his wife.

"I had a dream," she told him, pulling the covers off her legs. "Molly needs our help."

"Listen, Helen. Hold on, okay?" She tried to stand, but immediately fell back onto the bed. "Helen?"

This time she managed to get to her feet. She crossed the room and leaned against the bureau, working to catch her breath.

"She needs us, Charlie."

Yeah, he thought. And we both need a doctor.

"How long have we . . ." Her voice trailed off as she raised an unsteady hand to brush the hair away from her face.

"It's nearly noon," he told her.

He stood and went over to her, guiding her back to the bed. "Sit, okay? For a minute at least, will you please sit?"

"She's in terrible trouble, Charlie." He put his arm around her waist as they sat down on the edge of the mattress. "I just know she is."

Charlie felt a hollow burning deep in his chest. He shut his eyes and there was Molly, coming after him at the pond. As long as he lived, he knew he would be seeing her that way.

"Helen, tell me what she did to you."

Helen shuddered and looked away. "It doesn't matter what she did. She couldn't help herself."

"Did she make you swallow something?" Charlie asked.

"It was like she was possessed," Helen persisted, her voice breaking. "Like she didn't really have any choice."

"Helen, just tell me. Did she make you swallow a small black ball?"

The way she looked at him, he didn't need to ask again. A tragic light shone like a beacon in her gray eyes. The blood drained from his heart.

"Me too," he told her. "Listen, do you feel sick? Does your stomach hurt?"

She nodded, tears forming.

"I think we need to get to a doctor, Helen. God knows what—"

"No doctors, Charlie. There isn't time for that."

"Helen."

"And no police either."

He tightened his hold on her. She leaned against him, her head upon his chest. He tried to think this through. "Suppose she's not going to the cabin? If we call the police, they'll send out a—"

"She'll be there, Charlie."

"Just because you had a dream, that doesn't mean—"

"I'm going to the cabin, with you or without you."

"Helen, you can barely stand up."

"What's the matter, Charlie?" she asked. "You're afraid, aren't you? I thought you were a tough guy, but you're not. You're not a tough guy, are you? Fuck. The little booger's hungry, isn't he?"

And then, bending slowly forward, she retched and shivered, and the black ball slipped from her mouth.

Wet and heavy, it nuzzled like a puppy against Charlie's crotch, until with a grunt of disgust he swatted it away. It bounced across the carpet, hit the wall and ricocheted off the dresser, coming to rest directly in front of his feet.

Chirping like a drowning bird, the ball began to quake and vibrate, wobbling back and forth. As Charlie watched in disbelief, the surface bulged and blistered, and finally split open. A small black arm appeared, a human arm no larger than a Q-Tip, wearing a tan glove on its tiny fist.

Waving in the air, the arm flexed and the hand gripped the lip of the opening, struggling to widen the hole. Just as the pea-sized head popped into view—a hairy little raisin with a laughing face—Helen vomited up another ball, and then a third.

Charlie cried out and went to push her away, but then his eyes snapped open and there he was, still leaning back against the headboard, Helen sleeping peacefully at his side.

It was a long, hysterical moment before he realized that it had all been a dream—the entire conversation, the black ball, the miniature man fighting to be born.

Everything.

Lord Christ.

Charlie felt a soft thunder in his throat. Sitting up, he let out a shaky breath. The room was perfectly silent, except for the sound of a lone housefly circling overhead.

3

As Molly dragged the girl out to the Winnebago, she saw a hyena slip behind the dumpster in the corner of the parking lot, its small head carried low, a limp squirrel clenched in its jaws. Giving the girl's pretty hair a brutal twist, she walked her straight into the side of the RV, bloodying her nose.

Ah, yes. Life in the wild.

"Open the door," she said over her shoulder to Eddie.

Eyes filled with static, a loopy smile on his face, Eddie set down half his beer and pulled the door open, reaching out to pat the girl's fanny as Molly shoved her inside.

"Get in there and keep her quiet," Molly told him. "Leave it," she added, as he went to collect the two six-packs on the ground. "And don't give me any more shit, or I swear I'll suck your eyes right out of your head."

Climbing up the steps, he turned and gave her another goofy grin. "That's not exactly your better self speaking, is it?"

She slammed the door in his face. Kicking the beer on her way by, she hurried around to the driver's side and jumped in, just as a rusty pickup pulled into the lot, the old lady behind the wheel glancing curiously in their direction.

The girl was screaming now, the RV rocking as Eddie wrestled her down. "Shut her up!" Molly yelled, starting the engine and shifting into gear.

"Okay, Mom," Eddie said. "Don't worry, we'll behave."

Molly turned onto the state highway, heading north. The girl let out a long, wailing moan, kicking at the walls. When Molly glanced back, she saw Eddie under her, holding her tight, one arm around her throat and the other between her legs. Beside them on the floor, Ben was lying as still as a mannequin, watching everything with a dizzy-eyed stare, a beatific smile on his bearded face. His girlfriend up on the bed was out cold, no doubt introducing herself to Uncle.

Enjoying all the excitement, the lizard was perched on the edge of the dinette table, its little paws busy as usual beneath its apron.

Let the cries of the captives reach Thy presence, Molly prayed. *For their bones shall soon be scattered like splinters of wood.*

Along the side of the roadway, a straggly column of refugees marched southward, old people and children, gaunt with famine and dressed in dusty rags. Fields of dry stubble and stone stretched unbroken to the bloodred pinnacles and buttes on the horizon beyond.

At the intersection just past Santa's Land, Molly turned onto a narrower two-lane road. Another forty-five minutes at the most, and they'd be at the cabin.

Tired of listening to the ruckus in the rear, she turned the tape deck and Sinatra back on, cranking up the volume.

A moment later the girl started screeching again, and then nearly broke free. Molly would've preferred waiting until they reached the cabin, but she decided to go ahead and do her, just to quiet her down.

Looking for a place to pull over, she drove for another couple miles before finally spotting a small parking area on the right, with two picnic tables and a barrel for trash. She parked the RV under a tall solitary myrrh tree and switched off the engine, leaving the tape playing, old Frank's me-to-you croon setting the mood.

As she climbed into the back, her belly rumbled and rolled, the three remaining seeds jockeying for optimal position, each eager to be exuded into the world. Shaking with spasms of what appeared to be laughter, Eddie had the girl pinned on the floor. Wild with fear, she looked toward Molly, silently pleading for help.

Molly shuddered and gagged, bringing up the lucky seed, spitting it into her hands. It turned out to be the damaged one, her father's, the tear in its side looking nastier than ever. Holding it close, Molly examined it, gently squeezing the sphere until the jagged gash pouted open.

The wound was like a tiny cunt, all pink and tender. She caught a delicate fragrance, sweet and raw, a dark taint redolent of death. When she slipped the tip of her finger in there, the slick walls eased apart and she could see inside, see the intricate play of prismatic light and kaleidoscopic flares, radiant with a glittering blaze of colors.

"Please," the girl begged, giving a soft mournful sob. "Let me go."

Molly leaned forward and pressed the ball against the girl's lips.

As Molly forced the seed home, the field hippie suddenly jackknifed to life, arching his back like a bow, digging his heels into the floor.

"Oh!" he cried, rocking rapidly back and forth on his head and feet, his hands curled like claws. "Oh!"

"Spooky freak," Eddie muttered, adjusting his grip on the struggling girl. "Must be having a flashback."

If He passes by, thought Molly, *who can turn Him away?*

4

Charlie was still sitting there, looking down at Helen, when the white fly landed on her forehead. The size of a dime, it darted across her brow, pausing to wash and preen where a tear lay in the corner of her closed eye.

Charlie shooed it away, the damn thing hovering over the bed like a minuscule buzzard. When it circled in for another pass, he swung and hit it in midair, and it clung to the back of his hand for a second, buzzing like a dentist's drill. Zipping off, it did a kamikaze dive straight for his nose, pulling up at the last instant to swoop down and disappear into the trash can beside the desk. The basket immediately began to hum and whir, a beehive alive with dozens of midget dynamos.

The more Charlie told himself that this was only a dream, the louder the sound became. With a nauseous foreboding—*Over here, you fuck!*—he slowly stood and walked toward the desk. Three-quarters of the way there, he stopped and leaned forward, peering down into the basket as if he were looking over the edge of a precipice.

Covering the bottom of the can, scores of pale flies swarmed and danced furiously across a stringy blue mass.

Without a second thought, Charlie grabbed the basket and left the room. A few of the bugs flew off, but the rest stayed put, burrowing frantically between the thin slithery strands.

Holding it at arm's length, Charlie carried the can through the house and out the back door. Crossing the patio, he saw Harley standing under the maple tree with his front paws up on the trunk, whining at something in the branches overhead. Taking a rock from the border of the garden, Charlie upended the basket on the lawn and set the stone on top of it, so that none of the flies could escape.

"What is it, boy?" he called, looking across the yard. As far as he could tell, the tree appeared to be empty. As far as he could tell, this wasn't a goddamn dream. "Hey, Harley?"

Wagging his tail, Harley let out a bark or two and circled the trunk, then came trotting toward the patio. Christ, Charlie thought. Suppose it's Molly up there?

Hanging in the sky above the house, the mid-afternoon sun seemed oddly swollen, a hollow tarnished shell, a sterile seed. A hot dry breeze swept across the lawn, and for just a moment Charlie thought he heard drums, a faint measured pulsing drifting on the wind.

And then the kitchen phone began to ring, harsh and shrill. Turning away, he hurried inside, holding the door open for Harley.

"Daddy? Hi, I've been trying to get you guys all day."

"Linda," Charlie said into the phone.

"Where've you been? I must've called a dozen times. Did you all go out or something?"

At first Charlie's thoughts were in such a jumble, he had no idea what to say to her. Clearing his throat, flinching at the pain, he stared out the window above the sink, the maple tree stirring lazily now in the strengthening breeze.

"Daddy?"

"I'm here."

"Listen, the reason I've been calling is the car's still broken, so it looks like we're not going to make it over for supper today after all. But since it's so late, you've probably already figured that out."

Charlie looked up at the kitchen clock.

Four-thirty.

Jesus. Another what? Five hours lost? Had he really slept that long?

"So, where were you guys?" asked Linda.

But wait . . .

"Supper?" Charlie said.

"Yeah, Dad. Me and Arthur and the kids, remember? A barbecue?"

"Today?"

"Well, it's Sunday, isn't it?"

158

A whole day gone, Charlie realized, an icy constriction shivering up his spine. Twenty-four hours.

What the hell had Molly done to them?

"Dad?"

"Honey, will you . . . Can you hold on a second?"

"Sure. Is something wrong over—"

Charlie set the receiver on the counter. As he left the kitchen, he could hear his daughter's tiny voice still talking to him.

Returning to the bedroom, he sat down beside Helen. She seemed much cooler now, and her breathing was quiet and regular.

"Helen?" he said, shaking her shoulder. "Helen, it's me."

She shifted onto her back, but stayed asleep, her eyes twitching some beneath the lids.

Suddenly, Charlie knew what he had to do. Somebody had to go after Molly, and that somebody was him.

He could make it up to the cabin in less than four hours.

What other choice was there? Call the police? Sure, and tell them exactly what?

That's correct, officer. She forced something down our throats and we slept for a day. The keys to the cottage are missing, along with the RV. Anything else you need to know?

There was no doubt in his mind that Helen would want him to go after Molly himself. Besides, if there was any trouble, he could always call the cops once he got up there, right?

He picked up the telephone on the night table.

"Linda? I want you to listen to me, okay?"

"What is it? What's wrong?"

"You need to get over here. Now."

"Daddy, I—"

"If the car's broken, then just borrow a neighbor's, or a friend's, or somebody's, because you have to get up here."

"Will you please tell me what's going on? Is it Mom? Is she in the hospital again?"

"No, no, she's not in the hospital. Nobody's in the hospital."

"Is something wrong with Molly?"

Charlie paused, closing his eyes against the dull ache in the back of his brain. For a moment he nearly told her everything.

"Linda, I have to go somewhere. You need to come home and watch your mother. She's—"

"What are you talking about?"

"Will you please listen? Okay? Will you listen?"

Silence.

"Your mother is sleeping. You have to come up here and stay with her. Leave the kids at your place, with Arthur. Okay? When you get here—Linda, just listen. When you get here, let her sleep. No doctors. Understand? No doctors. Just let her sleep. She'll be fine."

"Where are you going?" Linda asked. "Where's Molly?"

"If she wakes up—"

"Dad?"

"—when she wakes up, tell her that I'm okay, and that I went after your sister. Will you do that?"

"Dad, you're scaring me. What's going on? You sound terrible."

"I'll explain it all later, I promise. Don't worry, everything will be fine. Just get over here."

"Okay, Dad. Okay. You don't want to tell me

anything? Then don't. I'll be there in twenty minutes. There's nothing wrong with the car, Arthur just wanted to stay home this weekend."

"I'll call you in a couple hours," Charlie told her. "Remember, as long as your mother seems comfortable, just let her rest. If she starts, well . . . vomiting, then . . ."

Then what?

"Hold on," Linda said. "She's sleeping, and she might vomit, and you're going to leave before I get there? Are you crazy?"

"Okay, I'll wait for you," he said. "Just please get in your car, right now, and drive up here."

"I'm on my way, Daddy."

"Great," he told her. "Drive carefully, you hear me?"

He hated lying to her like that, but there was no way he could stay and wait for her. She'd never let him go once she got here, and to tell the truth, he wasn't sure he'd have the strength to leave.

Helen still seemed to be sleeping peacefully. He tried to wake her one final time, brushing her hair back off her brow and saying her name. When he felt for her pulse, it was strong and clear.

He told himself that he shouldn't worry about her, that at the slightest sign of trouble Linda would be on the phone to Rescue. He told himself, again, that he didn't really have any choice about leaving, at least none that he could see.

He had to go after Molly, and the sooner he left, the better.

He sat there on the bed for several minutes more, watching Helen sleep, thinking how much better he would feel if she were coming along.

"I'll find her, Helen," he promised, leaning down to kiss her cheek. "Don't you worry, I'll find her."

Getting slowly to his feet, he walked over to the closet and grabbed his deer rifle off the top shelf, along with a box of shells. Taking a last look at Helen, he turned and left the room.

"Harley, let's go!" he called out in the kitchen, but there he was already, waiting by the door.

Charlie was putting the rifle on the floor in the back of the car when he felt something stirring in his shirt pocket. Reaching in, he pulled out the small black lizard skull that Molly had given him the other night.

Squiggling in his hand, it shifted about until it stared directly up at him, and Charlie saw that it wasn't the skull after all, it was the face from that dream—the face on the tree—giving him a jeering grin as it teetered forward and nipped at his palm, its tiny pin teeth pricking his skin.

Dropping it onto the driveway, Charlie crushed it beneath his heel, silencing its little outraged cries.

With Harley in the backseat he drove down the road about fifty yards, did a U-turn, and parked on the shoulder. Ten minutes later, as soon as he saw Linda's car pull into the driveway, Charlie started the car and left.

5

Farmland, orchards, dark wooded hills. Cars coming toward them and slipping by, the narrow two-lane highway unraveling ahead. Animal pancakes frying on the pavement.

"Lost?" Eddie went. He tapped the side of his head with his fist, as if to unstick a thought. "You're kidding me, right?"

Molly wanted to reach back in her blood and dream. All her bones were soft and black, all her organs ringing. She felt like a ripe fruit about to fall from the Tree. The Hungry Woman's harrowing cries swept across these fields, shadows fleeing from a ravenous sun.

Acting of its own volition, the fifth seed suddenly came alive in her belly, spinning like a top. She had no other option but to bring it up, keeping one eye on the road as she shuddered and gagged, Eddie kindly reaching over to catch the little monkey in his hands.

"I'm wet with love," he said gently, cradling the trembling sphere in his lap. "I can barely contain myself."

Inside a single chestnut there sleeps a hundred trees, branches spread against the sky. An entire clan might spring from the speck of fluid glistening on the tip of a man's cock. But nothing can compare to the bounty to be harvested from this sweet kernel.

Nothing.

As the RV rounded the next bend, Molly eased down on the brakes, checking the rearview mirror for traffic. Up ahead, a young girl was bicycling toward them on the side of the road. Ten, maybe eleven years old, not long away from her mother's breast.

"It must've known she was coming," Eddie said. "You have no idea how clear that makes everything."

Lifting the seed, he rested his hands on the dash, the black orb continuing to shimmy as it pressed itself against the windshield.

"See that?" he said. "It wants her. Its little heart has a hard-on. A real banger."

Slowing the Winnebago even further, she squinted at the approaching girl. *I lie down trusting in your darkness, Uncle,* she prayed. *For I know that even now you are here.*

Checking the mirror once again, and finding the road as empty behind them as it was ahead, Molly pulled the RV onto the shoulder. Shifting into park, she engaged the emergency brake and left the engine running.

"Get in back," she told Eddie, opening her door. "You can do her, if you want."

Eddie brought the seed to his mouth and kissed it. He liked his fun, there was no denying that. "Pinch me," he said.

Climbing out of the RV, Molly took note of the girl's bright red swimsuit, her long blond ponytail, her limbs so bare in the afternoon sun. When she tried to escape by riding across the road, Molly chased after her and knocked her to the blacktop.

Her pretty face was unscarred by this world, without evidence of corruption or sin. There were tiny chips of blue sky reflected in each of her frightened eyes. Gathering the crying girl in her arms, Molly carried her over to the RV, where Eddie was waiting with the side door open.

Throwing the kid inside, Molly climbed up front and put the Winnebago in gear. As Eddie wrestled the girl to the floor, she pulled the RV onto the road.

And so—six seeds and six people—the sowing was now complete.

Aileen sobbing quietly on the bunk, palming her tears as they fell, her head cocked, listening intently to a voice coming out of the sky. Ben still on the floor, breathing with hoarse expirations, a giant twitch running through his body every several seconds. Kim curled in a tight ball beside him, awaiting animation, silent except for an occasional whimper of terror. Eddie with the little girl, holding her tight, helping her along.

Plus me, Molly thought.

And Uncle . . .

CHAPTER ELEVEN

Quiet, Pudzie," he said, stepping off the path and into the shadows.

There was a light shining inside Meru's hut. Soft voices came shifting through the window. Creeping closer, Sibatia strained to hear.

"Dick dust . . . nerve block . . . memory balm. . . " someone said derisively. "Can you believe this crap?"

"Keep looking," a second voice replied, a woman's voice. "There has to be *something* decent."

Imagine, a woman here in the grove. And an American at that. What next? A McDonald's in the village square?

Intrigued, Sibatia left the shelter of the trees, Pudzo padding silently after him.

"Did you say dick dust?" the female asked. "Maybe you should grab some. It couldn't hurt."

Offended, Pudzo gave a low growl. Hushing him with a sharp gesture, Sibatia hesitated for a moment before approaching any nearer.

"Did you hear that?" the woman asked. "Just now?"

"Sounded like the old man's ghost to me, coming to get you."

"You didn't hear anything?"

"Actually, I think he said your name."

Joke all you want, Sibatia thought. Over the past few days, half a dozen people at least had spotted Meru's spirit wandering through the fields and village alleyways.

"I can't find shit," the male said disgustedly. "We waited too long. Somebody beat us to all the good stuff."

Silently, Sibatia moved toward the window.

Rolfe and Anne, weren't those their little names? Saint Rolfe and Saint Anne, humanitarian wonder workers from halfway around the globe. Peeking inside, he saw Anne kneeling on the floor, searching beneath Meru's bed, while Rolfe shifted through the paraphernalia on the shelves.

Thieving fools.

If he killed them, the villagers would likely assume that they had vanished on one of their frequent tours of the countryside. He would be finished with his work here long before anyone would grow suspicious, so he had no reason to be concerned on that account. He could kill them, taking his time with the female of course, then offer their healthy white flesh to the Angel.

Or, he could simply let them be.

"Lizard balls . . . root rot . . . more memory balm . . . brain wash?" the American recited, reading the labels on Meru's jars. "Here's another good one. Seed hardener."

Okay, so he'd kill them.

Walking toward the doorway, he gave Pudzo a sharp crack on the skull with his heel. "Bones on the hoof, boy. Hungry?"

Stepping into the light of the lantern, he cleared his throat.

"I know where he hid some things," he told the two do-gooders. "Special things, before he died."

"Do you, now?" Rolfe replied, exchanging a glance with Anne. "And where's that?"

"Under a tree," Sibatia said, thinking, *If I felt like it, I could suck their spines dry.* "Not far from here."

Getting off her knees and moving to stand before him, Anne displayed her best American smile. "Can you show us?"

Sibatia shrugged, as did Pudzo.

"Yes, no problem," he told them. "For five dollars."

"It better be worth it," Rolfe declared, reaching for his wallet.

"How about seven?" Sibatia amended.

"Sure, we can parley, pal," Rolfe agreed, handing over the money. "Christ, what's with these people?"

Slipping the bills into his pouch, Sibatia turned and left the hut. He led the Americans across the lawn and into the woods, whistling his mother's favorite lullaby softly to himself, the one she sang almost constantly during his second year in her womb. "Oh, the green bough blossoms . . ."

In a matter of moments they were standing at the base of the black gum tree.

"What is it?" Anne asked in disbelief.

"Not what—*who?*" Sibatia answered. "And frankly, I'd just as soon not go into details."

Knocking her to the ground, he pressed his hands

over her heart and silenced her first, then took care of the boyfriend.

"Settle down, shitcakes," he told them.

Making feeble motions with their arms, the pair of them convulsed and sputtered helplessly. Leaving them where they lay, with Pudzo happily lapping at the female's urine-soaked crotch, Sibatia approached the Angel.

Rising toward heaven, from glory to glory, she carried her beauty well. Rosy and contented, she was already coming to fruition.

Stepping forward, Sibatia touched her warm flank, a sinuous tremor coursing through the purpled flesh. Here we all are, he thought. Together.

It was a strangely emotional moment for him.

A grisly array of partially utilized entrails and appendages rose above him, a confection of assorted innards and gobbetty slops, suet and lace-edged rags of tissue. A profusion of wriggling antennae and thicker rudimentary pedicels sprouted to the right, multibranched extrusions seeping a nacreous paste. Bringing one of the spiracled stalks to his mouth, Sibatia sucked for a moment, the sorcerous sputum sweeter than any honey found on Earth.

Nutritious too.

Much refreshed, he circled the Angel, admiring her considerable charms. The swollen cushiony membranes mapped with dark veins, the billowy polyps secreting a drizzle of bloody dew, the upwelling pillows and slack white bladders, the squirmy udders and other Unclely crud.

Returning to his starting point, Sibatia sank his fingers into a patch of spongy sweetmeat and began to climb, detouring around a gauzy swatch of trans-morphing child-flesh. A man's head cranked about to stare at him as he reached up to grasp a glutinous half-peeled breast and a knotted hank of hair. Disturbed, the Angel shifted slightly, a soft sigh escaping from the aperture on her crown. A pleasant yeasty scent flooded the air as Sibatia scaled her sleek pulpy shoulders, his root stiffening in his shorts as he pressed himself closely against her.

Reaching the top at last, he gripped the slick lip of the hole and peered into the Angel's womb. Resting on the floor of the large chamber, puffed globes like lacquered sacks of wet meal stirred with a life of their own, lumpy clumps of brains, dreaming away.

Sibatia's hesitation was momentary. As eager as a schoolboy, he swung his legs over the edge and lowered himself down.

PART 3

The world set free

CHAPTER TWELVE

∽

1

With a whole forty-five minutes to kill before supper, Marshall and Steve decided to take a canoe out, and Howie figured he might as well go along. If he hung around the lean-to, Abrams was bound to find something for him to do, like collecting firewood, or policing the area, or maybe retying every loose knot in camp.

"What's this for, Doaks?" Marshall asked, making a grab for the towel Steve had tucked under his arm. "You planning on falling in?"

They were crossing the baseball field, and Steve stopped right at second. He shook his head sadly, giving Howie a see-the-shit-I-have-to-put-up-with look.

"Eat my leek," he told Marshall. "Feed, and be fat."

"You wish," Marshall replied. "Anyway, I thought that was Howie's job."

With deliberate care, Steve unfolded the towel. "Stoop, and bend thy knee," he said, revealing a magazine. "Behold."

There was a naked woman on the cover, holding her tits out and smiling. YELLOW WOMEN it said above her. And in smaller print, *Singapore Slave Markets—a Yen for Pleasure.*

"Where'd you get that?" Howie asked.

"I found it," Steve said.

Marshall leaned forward for a closer look. "Yeah, right. Where?"

"In McPherson and Doyle's cabin," Steve nonchalantly replied. "Under Doyle's bunk."

A moment of stunned silence greeted this news. McPherson and Doyle were the two oldest Scouts in the troop, both of them Eagles, both of them prone to committing random acts of violence upon their fellow campers.

"I seriously doubt it," Marshall finally said. "Even you're not that nuts, Doaks."

Steve shrugged, carefully refolding the towel around the magazine. "I had to take a dump during lunch today, right? Remember I left? Well, since everybody was in the dining hall, I went over to their cabin and looked around a little. No big deal."

"Doyle will kill you," Howie said. "He'll hang you upside down from the flagpole and fill you full of arrows."

"Nice imagination you have there, Campbell. Very nice." Steve shrugged again, obviously enjoying himself. From his shirt pocket he casually took out a half-empty pack of Marlboros. "Found these too. You got your lighter with you?"

"Yeah," said Howie. "I've got it."

"Well, I don't know about you nimrods," Marshall went, "but I'm way too young to die."

Steve laughed and turned back toward the cabins.

"Hey, Doyle!" he shouted. "Marshall Kendall has your magazine."

Marshall had this funny hair that was so coarse it almost always stood up on top of his head, and when he heard Steve yelling, it seemed to stick up even higher. He took a swing at Steve, and then one at Howie for good measure, and then the three of them ran hooting across the ballfield, Howie letting go with his patented Tarzan yell.

"Holy shit!" he said, feigning true terror. "Look who's after us now."

"Drop dead, Campbell," Marshall told him as they slowed to a walk again and took the short cut behind the crafts shed. "You guys are both out of your minds."

"Thou thing of no bowels thou!" Howie replied, borrowing one of Steve's lines. "Thy lips shall sweep the ground."

"Yeah? And your lips can sweep my ass."

Feinting and then quickly closing in, Marshall caught Howie in a headlock. When Steve jumped on, all three of them fell into the ferns alongside the path. Howie eventually ended up on top, but Marshall and Steve were pretty much holding each other down.

"Say Uncle," Steve went, "and I'll let you up."

"Okay, okay. Quit trying to hump me," Marshall answered. "Uncle!"

Untangling himself, Steve retrieved the magazine, having conscientiously set it aside before leaping onto Marshall. "Onward, thou beef-witted cowards."

Because it was just before supper, the lakefront was busier than usual. The canoe racks were empty and they had to settle for one of the green wooden rowboats. While Marshall and Howie each manned

an oar, Steve sat up front and traded insults with the
swimmers on the dock, a bunch of dorks from the
other Scout troop sharing the camp this week.

"Which one of you girls farted?" he asked them.
"Doth thine other mouth call me?"

Out past the raft, he emptied the pack of cigarettes
onto the bench. "Nine," he announced. "Three each."

"Let's have one," Marshall said. "Soon as we get
away from this crowd."

All boaters were to more or less remain at this end
of the lake, but if you hugged the shore, you could
usually put some extra distance between you and the
camp without one of the patrol leaders waving you
back in. Rowing steadily, matching Marshall stroke
for stroke, Howie watched the waterfront recede. Fifty
yards out, a canoe full of geeks from Troop 84 zipped
by, threatening to ram them, before veering off and
heading for shore.

The water was clean and still, cold even now in
midsummer. According to camp lore, the lake was one
of the deepest in the entire state. Taking a break,
Howie peered down into the sky, a passing plane
dividing the blue air below them with a thin white
trail.

"I had this incredibly weird dream last night,"
Steve said.

Marshall quit rowing as well, pulling in his oar.
"Don't tell me, okay? I don't want to know about it."

"I dreamt that—"

"Don't tell me!" Marshall said. He reached for one
of the three cigarettes Steve had left sitting on the
bench. "I'm tired of hearing about your stupid
dreams."

"Well, excuse me, Ken Doll, sir." Steve handed Howie his Marlboro and took the last one for himself. "How about a light, Campbell, my man?"

Fishing out his Bic, Howie looked back toward camp. Deep or not, Lake Union really wasn't much more than a large pond. They were already nearly halfway across. Of course, come Tuesday morning, when he and a few other fools in the troop set out to earn their mile-swim merit badge, it was going to seem wider than the Pacific, especially after the first lap.

"Say hey to Alesha Shea," Steve read, settling back and opening the well-thumbed magazine. "An accomplished visual artist, originally from the tiny island of Nagoyato, her mission in life is to become an ambassador of goodwill among people of all nations."

Giving Howie back his lighter, Marshall went over and sat beside Steve. "Hey, Alesha Shea." Furrowing his brow in concentration, he expertly exhaled a stream of smoke from the corner of his mouth. "What's with the tattoo down there?"

"Oh, that?" Steve was already turning the page. "That's Japanese for Steve. She's crazy about me."

Leaning over the side, smoking contentedly, Howie spotted a twelve-inch trout sliding out of the boat's shadow, coasting across the sky, a fish larger than any he'd ever caught in his life. When he let go with a gob of spit, the trout rose for a moment, lazy but curious, before thinking better of it and continuing on its way.

"Hey, you guys," he said. "Look at this fish."

"Keep it down, Campbell, okay?" Marshall went. "We're busy over here."

"All right, boys. All right, pay attention now. Here's

177

one." Steve moved the magazine so that Marshall could no longer see it. When Marshall made a grab for it, Steve told him to relax.

"Just hold on, Kendall, you're drooling all over your uniform. Get a grip on yourself. Try both hands."

Turning the magazine around, he held out a full-page photo of a pretty Oriental woman, long black hair and a nice smile, lying on her back with her legs up and wide apart, showing everything. The whole works.

Marshall swore softly and then started coughing, a cloud of smoke erupting from his lungs.

"Gentlemen, for one hundred points," Steve said, flipping the magazine back around. "A bodybuilder and nursing student from Hidako, a perfectionist who likes to have fun. Please tell me, quote, 'What turns Tomako on?' Unquote."

For a few seconds everything was still. The boat rocked gently, the laughter and shouts from the shore muffled by distance, sounding hollow and bell-like. When Howie tried locating the trout again, the only thing he could see in the water was his own face looking back at him.

"I give up," Marshall finally said.

"Howie?" Steve asked. "For one hundred points, what turns Tomako on?"

"I'm gonna say Boy Scouts," Howie guessed. "American Boy Scouts."

"Well, not quite, How. I'm sure we're high on her list, though." Steve consulted the magazine. "The correct answer is, and I quote, 'A bottle of rice wine and a cherry-blossom moon. That's all it takes for me.' Unquote."

There was another lengthy silence as Steve showed the photo again. Howie stared, the boat swaying beneath them, holding them safe above the cold dark depths.

"Boys, I think I'm in love," Steve said quietly, turning the page with a sigh.

Marshall dropped his cigarette in the water and leaned closer, squinting at the next woman on display.

Taking up the oars, Howie dipped them in, moving the boat in a slow circle. He was facing the south shore of the lake when he saw the RV pulling into the yard of one of the summer homes over there. As he watched, the side door of the camper suddenly flew open and a woman jumped out and fell sprawling onto the ground.

"'Anyone who doesn't believe in fairy tales,'" Marshall read, "'should meet—'"

"Look at that," Howie said.

As the woman struggled to her feet, some guy leapt from the front of the RV and knocked her down again. Then another woman climbed out, and she and the guy started fighting the first woman, dragging her toward the house.

"Call 911," Steve said. "And remember, you *can* make a difference."

But it wasn't funny.

If you listened closely, you could hear the woman screaming.

2

One of these days, Uncle would find her and exchange her brain. Newly outfitted, she would explore strange times and worlds of alternate possibilities. He would give her a new heart as well, and a new womb more suitable to his needs.

He would give her a dream or two, then take them away.

Standing before the bay window, she looked out over the empty lake. The armada of Scouts had returned to shore for their supper. Once when she was very young, her father had taken her and her sister out fishing in a canoe, and they had capsized because she and Linda had begun fighting. In December, if the snow held off long enough, the lake froze into a single smooth sheet and you could skate for an entire afternoon without crossing your own tracks. For Christmas her mother liked to carry a tree to the center of the lake and decorate it with popcorn chains for the birds. On the Fourth of July her father always took them out on the water, filling the sky with streaking bottle rockets and whistling flares.

"I'm telling you," Eddie said behind her. "The little sweetie's not going to make it."

He had this smile now like a scar. When he spoke, tiny flecks of black tissue sprinkled from between his lips. There was a fresh bite mark on his neck, a screaming bloody ring.

"I think she's leaving us." Holding up his hands, he

examined them closely for a moment, as if they had just sprouted on the ends of his arms. "I think it's time for her dirt nap."

Molly's head felt all clammy. She tried to blink away the red haze in her mind. Turning from the window, she pushed past the hippie girl jabbering to herself in the center of the room.

On the black Naugahyde couch, the child lay suffering, barely able to breathe. She thrashed and flailed feebly, too weak to sit up. The seed within her was wasting no time, ravaging her small life apace. As Molly leaned over the sofa, the girl's unfocused eyes fixed on her for an instant, wild with fear.

"Mommy?" she gasped. *"Mommy!"*

The day is too long for such gentle souls, the night too dark and empty. Still, when the Red Wind blows, every blossom on the Tree must tremble.

"It's beginning," Molly said, straightening and glancing around the room. On the floor in front of the TV, Kim and Ben were curled side by side, both staring blankly up at the ceiling. Aileen was dancing now, waving her arms and dipping in slow circles, following the lead of the lizard capering nimbly between her feet. "It's beginning for all of us."

Eddie's gawping grin momentarily faded, a swift twitch of concern worming its way across his face. "Already?"

Lifting up her T-shirt, Molly showed him the hole in her belly. An inch or so below her navel, the opening was roughly the size of a dime. Lipless and unpuckered, the perfectly round orifice flexed slightly wider as Molly touched it with her fingertips, lightly caressing its rim.

"Already," she told him. His crazed smile flashed again as she inserted her finger deep into her stomach. "For all of us."

And sure enough, when Eddie raised his own shirt, he found a spongy pale patch of transformed tissue directly beneath his belly button, a tiny pouting mouth just beginning to form.

"Maybe I should put some ointment on this." He laughed, teasing the grainy blister with his thumb. "What do you think?"

Should she warn him? Molly wondered. Should she try to explain at least some of what was happening?

"Jee-sus," Eddie went, pinching the fleshy berry. "That feels pretty good."

"By the time this is over with," Molly told him, "we'll be nothing more than a heap of bones."

Eyes beaming with strange force, he looked up at her, his voice tight with excitement. "Yeah, some fat trip we're on, right? It really boggles."

When he reached for her, she stepped back, a little surprised by the measure of his need.

"We're out on the frontier here, aren't we?" he said. "We're crossing over into uncharted terrain."

He went for her again, but she slapped his hands away.

"How about we play a few rounds of stinkfinger?" he suggested, pointing down at her belly. "You know, while we're waiting for the fun to start."

The poor fool was frightened to death, Molly realized. Old dogs have more dignity.

"Let me get something from the RV," she told him. "Then we'll try a couple things."

"My heart leaps," he said, casually stroking the

growth beneath his shirt. "Thick rich fluids begin to rise and flow."

Leaving the cabin, Molly recalled the tale of Uncle Dry Skull's jism, a story Sibatia had told her more than once. Betrayed by the Grandfathers, flayed and hung by his neck from the lowest limb of the World Tree, his spunk had spurted for nine days and nights from his stolid member, the Red Aunts gathering every last drop. One hundred tall urns had been filled before the Grandfathers realized their folly and cut him loose, one thousand young Aunts made heavy with his spawn.

Outside, the sun was humming with light. Flitting ahead across the lawn, the lizard turned cartwheels and somersaults as it scampered toward the lake.

How long had it been, Molly asked herself, since she'd found the little demon lying in her bed? It could have been a year ago, or just yesterday. Her life between then and now had become one long dream.

She knew she must be nearly dead, but the thought of what awaited her tempered her spirit. A strange new happiness stirred within her now, a constant organic thrill, like electricity almost, purring in her belly and turning her skull to glass. Her body was softening, letting itself go. Little by little Uncle's gentle warmth was melting every frozen lock within her.

From the RV she collected the tin of wafers, the pliers, and the carving knife. Walking down to the lake, in no hurry to return inside the cabin, she found the lizard crouched on the shore, devouring a frog, glistening crumbs of torn flesh and gristle spilling from the reopened hole beneath its skirt.

Looking away, out across the face of the water, she thought once again of how her father would row out to the center of the lake, every July Fourth, filling the black crystal sky overhead with a shower of starbursts, each hissing speck of light falling like a bright seed to meet its reflection rising in the dark water below.

3

Keen for union, Eddie Starling sat beside the little girl on the sofa and watched the hippie babe work out.

She'd settled into this herky-jerky dance routine, stretching and squatting, her arms reaching way up and her legs pumping like pistons beneath her baggy dress, climbing apparently, her cupped hands grabbing at the air as she pulled herself higher. Puffing and gasping, every so often she'd pause for a second to catch her breath, then start in again crazier than ever, peering down at her feet like something might be overtaking her.

Kneading his temples, trying to get some blood flowing into his brain, Eddie considered the possibility of putting his root right to her. With these alpha-female types, the sooner you get them tuned up and quivering, the better. He could do her first, then try Kimmy on for size, and save the littlest one for last.

Her hands jigging in the air as she writhed on the couch, the kid was staring up at him now, creaking like a tiny bird. Oh, the sweet itches she aroused.

Getting to his feet, his bones vibrating like tuning forks, Eddie crossed the room and knocked Aileen down with a blow to the side of her neck. "Hey, Stuff," he said. "Let's get sticky."

She rolled over onto her back, her breath whistling in and out. "Oh, you," she whispered, liquid eyes dark with yearning. "Come into my shade."

Say what? Eddie thought, dropping to his knees beside her. Pulling off her skirt, he slid her undies down and unfastened his pants.

"You lovable cow you," he told her, ripping open her blouse. "You bring out my kinder, gentler side."

As he slipped into her, she growled and clutched him so nice and tight, he didn't even mind the stench of patchouli oil and beans.

"Pretty tasty, eh?" he said, working himself in deep. She winced and her head lolled back and she did this little spasm thing down there, really coming alive.

"Go ahead, haul it all out," he told her. Oh, the wonder, the drama. Heady, heady, Stuff.

And then who should come crawling over but old Mister Natural.

"Get off," he wheezed, rocking forward onto his elbows, too weak to do much more than lift his head. "Get off her."

Keeping his rhythm going, Eddie let out a harsh chuckle. "Don't get your fur up, hairface. Just sit back and enjoy the presentation. Try to look at the larger picture, okay? I'll get to you in a minute."

He shook his head. This sort of thing went on dismayingly often.

Moaning deliciously, Stuff pulled him closer still, seeking a little comfort for her bones.

"I think your boyfriend has some major hang-ups," Eddie told her. "Maybe it's a self-esteem problem, or it could even be that he's on drugs."

She began laughing then, and she kept on laughing as the spaghetti-thin tendril snaked out of her mouth. She laughed as it looped through the air, the tip suddenly darting up to plant a stinging kiss in the center of Eddie's forehead, stabbing through his skull and blossoming in his brain, a thousand sprouting fibrils instantly piercing every thought.

His spinal column flared with a fine golden fire, and it was by this soft light that he saw everything unfolding.

With a long hooting cry, she opened herself to him. A spidery web of fissures spread across her belly, patterning her flesh with an intricate brocade as scores of tiny pale shoots appeared on her breasts, little dancing spermies poking free.

"Come into my shade," she said again. "Let it happen."

And then her torso came neatly undone, from sternum to crotch, her skin flaking back in layered sheets, curling to either side, revealing the wet bits and gut strings within. Loose blood spurted all over the place.

"Don't you people have any self-control?" he asked.

A fuggy putridness wafted upward into Eddie's face as he spotted the juice-shiny gelatin ball nestled comfortably among her innards. Wrapped in a tangle of glassy veins and braided filaments, the slick black sphere swiveled and pulsed, humming like a happy little beehive.

The simplest way to get to know someone is to see how they die.

Okay, okay. Big deep breaths for everyone.

4

"Footboy," Steve Doaks said to Marshall Kendall. "Your virginity breeds mites, much like a cheese."

Howie was lying on his bunk, working on a letter to his folks. He didn't have a clue what to tell them. He'd never written to his parents before. All of a sudden, it was like they were complete strangers. But the funny part was, he actually missed them.

"Me think'st thou art a general offense, and every man should beat thee," Steve said to Marshall.

"Beat this, Doaks," Marshall replied.

Steve was sitting on his trunk, paging through his book of Shakespearean insults, a gift from his father, who taught high school English. Marshall was over on his bunk, struggling with the leather moccasins he'd been making all week, not exactly successfully.

"Thou tickle-brain. Thou unwholesome humidity." Steve turned the page. "Thou eater of broken meat."

"Eat this, Doaks," Marshall said.

On the other bunk in the lean-to, Eric Montoya's bunk, two freckle-faced eleven-year-olds were studying Pinhead Doyle's dirty magazine. Every once in a while one of them would giggle or whisper something, but mostly they were quiet. With the canvas flap down, the lean-to was growing stuffier by the minute, thick with the stench of dirty laundry, wet towels, sweat, and stale farts. And behind everything you could still smell Eric's vomit, always a trace, which wasn't surprising considering the guy must've hurled a dozen times before they finally shipped him home the other day.

"Thou art a boil, a plague sore, an embossed carbuncle in my corrupted blood," Steve read. "I would rather be a dog, and bay at the moon, than be such a one as thee."

Hi Mom and Dad, Howie wrote. *Sorry I haven't written to you yet, but I've been very busy here. I've already earned two merit badges. Archery and First Aid. On Tuesday, I do my mile swim.*

Great start, but now what? He'd been at camp since last weekend, and this was all he could come up with? Setting down his notebook and pencil, he pulled his duffel bag out from under his bunk. When he zipped it open and took out the box of taffy his parents had sent him in the mail yesterday, everybody stopped what they were doing and looked over at him.

"You guys are such mooches," he said, holding the box out so that everyone could help themselves.

"Read your handbook," Marshall said, unwrapping his taffy and popping it into his mouth. "You should always remember your fellow Scouts. It's your duty."

"Thou itch of nature," Steve told him. "Thou misshapen Dick."

Giving up on the moccasins, Marshall tossed them into his black footlocker. Moving to the front of the lean-to, he took out his pocketknife and started flipping it off his fingertips, the blade sticking upright in the floor just about every time.

"Sorry, girls," Steve said, going over to the two Webelos on Montoya's bunk and closing the magazine. "I'm afraid your fifteen minutes are up."

Reluctantly getting to their feet, one of the boys

fished a crumpled dollar bill out of his pocket and handed it to Steve.

"It's been a pleasure doing business with you," he told them, lifting the corner of the canvas flap and ushering them outside. "Come back anytime."

"Okie-doakie, Doaks," Phil Abrams said, appearing out of nowhere, poking his pimply patrol-leader face right up close to Steve's. "Thank you, I most certainly will."

Pulling back the flap, he hooked it tight to the side wall.

"Kendall, I've told you a hundred times, you retard, no knives inside. You wanna play mumblety-peg? Fine. Do it in the freakin' ground, not into the floor of the freakin' lean-to. I don't know what you think you're doing here," he said, addressing the pair of Webelos now, "but this little party's over. Get back to your own patrol."

Thanks for the delicious taffy, Howie added to the letter. *See you next Sunday. Love, Me.*

"Let's go, you three," Abrams said. "It's time to assemble."

"Yes, sir," Steve said, waiting until Abrams's back was turned before giving him the modified one-finger salute. "We gladly obey your every command."

"You know, I'm seriously thinking of pulling a Montoya," Marshall said, putting his knife away. "Eat some deer shit, or something, puke my brains out until my folks come up and get me, and just like that, I'm out of here. Home-free."

Under Abrams's watchful eye Beaver Patrol formed into a ragged line in front of its assigned lean-tos. On either side the other patrols in the troop were doing the same, Mustangs and Bobcats, Lions, Hawks and

Bears. It was Evening Activity Time at old Camp Keewaydin, time once again for Troop 52 to march forth and defend its honor.

"All right, you Brownies, let's move," Abrams said, leading the way down the path.

The boys sang out as they walked along, competing with the other patrols.

> "One, two, three-and-a-half,
> Won't you kiss my flabby ass?"

"Knock it off, Beavers," Abrams called back over his shoulder.

> "Six, seven, eight, nine,
> Won't you bite my big behind?"

Troop 84 was waiting for them on the main field, just as they had been for the past two evenings. Since they were heading home to Connecticut in the morning, tonight's game of Capture the Flag would be the last. The score was now tied, one all, and it was time for the title match.

"We should play Messengers and Interceptors instead," Howie said.

Marshall nodded in agreement. "Yeah, with paint grenades."

> "Thirteen, twelve, eleven, ten,
> Won't you tickle my rear end?"

"I'm warning you," Abrams growled under his breath, bringing the patrol to a halt alongside the Mustangs. "Doaks. Campbell. Knock it off."

Over near the flagpole, Pinhead Doyle and Meathead McPherson, along with old man Barker, the Scout Master, were busy rehashing the rules and boundaries with their counterparts from 84. As usual, Barker was doing most of the talking, his beefy red face flapping like the flag overhead.

"Sure you don't want to come with us tonight, Ken Doll?" Steve asked Marshall, keeping his voice low.

"No, thanks. I'm in no rush to spend the rest of my life dead."

The pregame powwow finished, Doyle and McPherson sauntered back toward the troop, Barker gimping along behind them, muttering to himself and shaking his head.

"Seriously," Steve said. "Somebody should put Barker away in a rest home. He's had it."

"Okay, listen up, men," the Scout Master said, hands on hips, back fairly straight, watery eyes sweeping the loyal ranks arrayed before him. "These candy-ass flatlanders are about to get their sweet little butts kicked, and I mean kicked good. We got the same boundaries tonight as last night, our territory being the pond side and theirs starting at the archery range, and so on. Me and Mr. Julio over there are refereeing this particular affair, just so there's no misunderstandings when we win. Now here's the deal. We beat them, and you all get an extra hour's swim-time tomorrow. They beat us, and what you get is a little hike up Rattlesnake Mountain before breakfast. Any questions?"

Steve raised his hand, but Barker ignored him.

"One more thing," the Scout Master said. "The man who brings in the opposing team's flag will

receive as a reward one half gallon of ice cream a day
for the next five days."

"What flavor?" Howie called out.

"There's only one flavor, Campbell. You know
that," Pinhead Doyle said. "Keewaydin Crunch."

"Yummy," Marshall went. "Ice cream in a can."

"Patrol leaders," Barker ordered. "Front and center."

The next few minutes were spent in consultation,
assigning duties and devising strategy. Defensive and
offensive squads were selected, guards and scouts
chosen and briefed. Possible routes of incursion into
enemy territory were discussed, sprinters and flankers
cautioned concerning likely sites of ambush. Additionally, Meathead McPherson took Howie, Steve,
and Marshall aside for a moment, to offer a little
personal advice.

"If you three screw up again?" he snarled. "Like last
night? I guaranfuckingtee you I'll be righteously
pissed."

Steve was about to say something, but Howie
punched him in the arm.

"That's right, girls," McPherson added. "Don't say
a word."

When Marshall let go with a loud fart, Meathead
appeared truly surprised. "Very constructive, Kendall. I'll get back to you later."

"Eat my leek," Steve told him. "Feed, and be fat."

McPherson just stood there for a few seconds,
looking at each of them in turn, before finally walking
away, shaking his head in disbelief.

"Okay, men," Barker announced. "Let's get
started."

With an enthusiastic cheer, the troop dispersed, scattering in every direction. As roving defenders, Howie, Marshall, and Steve could pretty much go wherever they wished. Marshall, though, decided to make himself into a spy, an infiltrator deep behind enemy lines.

"Sure you don't want to come along?" he asked.

"Next time," Howie told him, but already Marshall was running off.

Taking up position behind the wood shop, Steve and Howie waited for the whistle to sound, signaling the start of the game. Steve produced a Marlboro and Howie pulled out his lighter.

"After McPherson and Doyle get through killing us," Howie said, "do you think our bodies will be shipped home in our footlockers?"

"Are you kidding?" Steve lit up, the smoke hanging in a small drifting cloud in front of him. "What bodies? There won't be anything left."

Finally, Barker gave the official signal, and the game began. Passing the cigarette back and forth, Steve and Howie sat quietly behind the shed, looking out across the lake at the summer house on the opposite shore, the one with the white RV parked in the yard.

"So, what time are we going tonight?" Steve asked.

Howie shrugged. "Right after lights-out, I guess."

5

As the day darkened outside the cabin's windows, Molly gathered the necessary supplies, finding the Wesson oil and the scissors in the kitchen, and the shaving cream and disposable razors in the bathroom cabinet. Returning to the family room, she pushed the furniture back against the knotty pine walls, her mother's wooden rocker and her Dad's recliner, the coffee table and the black couch holding the sleeping girl. Everything felt oddly weightless in her hands, like so many cheap cardboard props on a second-rate set.

Lying on the rug in the center of the room, Aileen was burgeoning nicely, her cadaver now sporting an assortment of pendulous growths. Rising several feet above her splayed torso, sinewy stalks swayed and shivered, droplets of blood like liquid rubies leaking from their nozzled tips. Fine, glistening webs stretched across her torn breasts and veiled her face, studded with opaque ruffled bulges and nubby pollen-filled projections.

The world waxes green in triumph through Him, Molly reminded herself. *Spirits flourish and creep through the leaves.*

Lifting the little girl off the couch, she placed her on the floor alongside the blossoming corpse. Then she coaxed the semiconscious Kim over and positioned her beside Ben.

While Eddie stripped the hippie, Molly removed Kim's clothes. Then she and Eddie both disrobed together, Eddie staring with obvious interest at the festering wound between her legs.

Opening the tin of wafers, she distributed three to everyone, the men eating theirs unassisted, while Molly first fed Kim and then the girl. Politely, they all sat as she in turn ate hers, sharing the final one with the lizard.

Pulling off the little girl's swimsuit, Molly noted once again how truly beautiful she was. Carefully, she brushed away the few grains of sand that clung like powdered sugar to her belly. Her pretty face was peaceful now, her small chest rising and falling steadily. Leaning close, Molly inhaled that special sweet scent that only young girls seem to have.

Picking up the scissors, she grabbed the blond ponytail and clipped it off, then began snipping at the remainder of the hair. When she started rubbing on the shaving cream, the girl fussed and squirmed, shivering like a frightened puppy until the wafers kicked in.

"Shhh . . . Time to rest, honey," Molly told her, taking up a razor. "Time to rest."

It didn't take long to shave and dry her head, revealing the small-boned frailness of her perfect skull. At her age, her tender body was just beginning to bud. Molly spread the oil gently onto her flesh, until every part of her was slick and shiny, front and back.

As she broke open the razor and removed the blade, a reverent silence fell over them all—Ben, Eddie, and Kim, who was wide awake now—even the lizard busily inspecting the proffered bounty of Aileen's corpse.

The girl flinched a bit during the first few slices, her

eyes fluttering as she let out a soft moan, the sound passing from her lips directly to Uncle's ears.

"Come into this house, You who have no foes," Molly recited. "Oh, Fairest One, come into this house and be with us."

Cutting deeply enough to cause significant bleeding, Molly carved the outline of a tree into the girl's chest and belly, a strong tree, one true enough to lift up the entire world.

"We see You not, Uncle," Molly declared, "and our hearts yearn after You."

As if in response, the girl's stomach visibly shifted and swelled.

"Hand me those pliers," Molly said after a moment, smiling over at Eddie. "And the knife."

6

For a second it was close.

The loud rush of gravel beneath the wheels shocked him awake, the car already drifting onto the grassy shoulder. Jerking the steering wheel sharply to the left, Charlie felt the Toyota's rear end begin to float.

Working the brakes, he gave the mirror a quick glance, just in case somebody was on his ass. The highway was empty, though, and he eased the car back into the slow lane.

This was crazy. He couldn't keep driving without taking some kind of break. It was a good ten miles yet to the St. Johnsbury exit, and another forty-five minutes after that before he reached the cabin. No way could he drive straight through. There was a rest area a few miles south of the exit, and he decided he'd better stop there.

Rolling the window down, he tried the radio, switching stations back and forth, but finding Rush Limbaugh on just about every other one. As he counted the miles, cars caught up with him and raced on by, the stars hanging low above the black mountains on both sides of the road.

Finally, just as he was about to pull over, he spotted the rest area up ahead.

There was only one car in the lot, plus two campers huddled together down at the far end. Parking near the picnic tables, Charlie sat for a moment, the sensation of motion slowly draining away. Cicadas sang in the dark trees around the tables as the Toyota's engine pinged softly beneath the hood.

Climbing from the car at last, Charlie opened the back door. With a weary groan, Harley jumped stiffly to the ground, stretching and scratching for a minute before wandering off across the grass.

Inside the comfort station, all the vending machines were locked behind a large metal gate. Well, so much for buying some coffee. After splashing cold water on his face in the john, Charlie headed back outside and found the phones.

"Yeah?" Arthur said in a sleep-thickened voice, finally answering after a dozen rings. "Who's this?"

"Arthur? It's me, Charlie."

"Christ, Charlie. Where the hell are you?"

"How's Helen? Is she okay?"

There was a pause then, as Arthur cleared his throat.

"She's over at Brattleboro Memorial, Charlie."

"What happened?"

"Linda wanted to bring her in. She's been over there a couple hours now."

"How bad is she?"

"Looked awright to me, Charlie," Arthur told him. "Once we got her awake and all, she seemed pretty good."

Appearing out of the trees along the edge of the lawn, Charlie watched a young man walking from the shadows into the light. Twenty, twenty-five years old, ponytailed and bearded, he was dressed in jeans and work boots, his chest bare. Carrying his T-shirt crumpled in his hands, he was using it to clean something off his fingers.

"Charlie, where the hell are you?" Arthur asked again. "Is Molly with you?"

From where he was sitting near the Toyota, Harley gave the guy a halfhearted bark.

"Linda's probably still at the hospital, right?" Charlie said.

"Last I heard, she was spending the night." Arthur recleared his throat. "She told me to tell you to call her over there."

"Okay, I will. Are the kids with you?"

"My sister's got 'em," Arthur said. "Hold on, and I'll get you the number for the hospital."

Harley barked again, louder this time.

"Fuck you, doggie," the guy said, still wiping at his hands. Then he looked over and saw Charlie standing at the phone.

Climbing into his car, a brand new BMW, he tossed the T-shirt into the backseat. Tires screeching, he swung the car around and drove off, keeping the headlights dark until he was out on the highway.

When Arthur returned, he read the number twice. "You gonna tell me what's going on?" he said.

"It's a long story, Art. Don't worry, you'll hear it, but not now."

"Call Linda, okay? Will you do that? Will you call the hospital?"

"Sure," Charlie promised. "I'll do it right now."

Hanging up, he dialed the number, and requested to speak with the head nurse on Helen's floor.

"Mr. Coughlin," a gruff voice greeted him. "I'm Curt Weston. How can I help you?"

Helen was nauseous, but sleeping peacefully. Her temperature was a little elevated, and they were waiting for the results of some blood tests.

"So far, though, I'd say she's in pretty decent shape," Weston concluded. "Mr. Coughlin, your daughter is here with her now. Would you like to speak—"

Thanking him quickly, Charlie hung up. He felt terrible, but he just didn't have the strength to face Linda right then.

Letting Harley into the back of the car, Charlie sat behind the wheel for a moment and closed his eyes. Listening to the crickets' chirring song, he tried to put everything from his mind.

Strangely soothing, the cadenced sound of the insects soon took on the quality of a simple tune, a few sibilant beats of a lullaby repeated again and again. Finally relaxing a little, Charlie let the melody carry him along.

He felt as if he'd been gone a long time, and when he came back from wherever it was, he found himself sitting on the ground, leaning against a tree. Bringing up a hand to shade his eyes from the glare, he stared in wonder at the woods around him.

Every tree was shimmering with spectral brightness, every bush and boulder brilliant with crystalline light. Sunbeams as iridescent as lasers sparkled through the canopy above, jeweled rays rippling the mottled air. A cascade of colors flooded everything, mirrored flares and diamond-pointed aureoles gilding every leaf and glasslike blade of grass.

Waist-high plants of silver and jade rose around him like exquisite sculptures. A breeze brought a delicate fragrance and a flickering of distant bells. Veils of emerald and polished gold shifted through the tall glowing trees as intricate mosaics pulsed and glittered across the luminous ground.

"Don't get too comfy, old man," a voice said behind him. "Every tree you see is a gallows. A gibbet cross."

Leaping to his feet, his heart surging, Charlie spun around and saw a naked black man hanging from the nearest branch, a gem-encrusted noose cinched snug about his swollen neck.

A dog's corpse dangled from a second rope beside him, fat white flies drinking at its open, opalescent eyes.

"Small world, ain't it?" the man said, giving Charlie a gap-toothed grin. Reaching up, he began undoing the knot, loosening it loop by loop. "Sorry if I startled you. I was just trying to get myself hard."

Charlie took a step back, thinking, *Here we go again.*

Thinking, *Wake up . . . Wake up now!*

"You're not going anywhere," the man told him. "Not this time."

Dropping to the ground, landing lightly on his toes, he started untying the dog's noose, raising his eyebrows and gesturing at the stubby pink erection poking between the dog's rear legs.

"True power is always heralded by great pain," he said, taking the dog in his arms and placing it gently on the rainbow-dappled grass. "As you will soon discover."

"You know all about Molly, don't you?" Charlie said. A viscera-deep cramp of fear stitched through him. "You know what's wrong with her, and you know where she is."

"You're not going to be able to save her, Charlie boy. She's my lovely now, not yours."

When the dog whimpered and rolled onto its back, the man leaned over and affectionately rubbed its belly.

"You, I just own a little piece of," he added, fixing his dull yellow eyes on Charlie. "But I've got my hooks sunk into every prime inch of that sweet bitch."

Stepping forward, Charlie kicked him in the balls as hard as he could.

With a sputtering cry, the scrawny black man fell to one knee, struggling for breath as he clutched his groin.

"Feel what you feel," he told Charlie, slowly getting back onto his feet. "Just don't lose sight of the Mystery."

Wake up, Charlie told himself. *Please wake up . . .*

But he wasn't going anywhere.

Not this time.

CHAPTER THIRTEEN

Labass! Sibatia swore, cursing his sore stones.

Imagine the nerve of that guy. Just his luck to go looking for the girl and find her father instead.

Leaning back, sinking into the Angel's dreamy softness, Sibatia sighed, recalling some of the more savory details of his session with the old man.

Determined sonovabitch, you had to give him that much. Dumb as a day-old turd, maybe, but he sure as hell was determined.

Speckled with knuckles and teeth, the wall of flesh before him was splattered with rosettes of raspberry-colored blood. Delicately poised, an adventurous brain was clinging to the glazed surface, writhing like a sack of snakes as it journeyed skyward. Just to its left, hinged slats slithered and flexed, oozing dollops of aromatic resin.

Gingerly, Sibatia stood, bending down for a moment to place a kiss on the bulging brow of the brain that had served as his pillow. The frail, whiplike tendrils scattered around the wall of the chamber quivered and throbbed in tandem, acknowledging his gesture. A chitinous scraping sound came from a nearby cluster of convoluted folds and looping crimson pipes, followed by a gasping sob and a muffled gurgle. For just an instant there was the faintest suggestion of many voices reaching out together, a susurration of lost souls babbling at the edge of a dream.

"Angel," Sibatia whispered. "We thank you for this gift."

Not wishing to overstay his welcome, he turned to leave, then hesitated in front of the nursery, admiring the brittle golden honeycomb arching across the wall. Each perfect cell held a miniature blue ball no larger than a robin's egg, one hundred newborn angels, one hundred sacred seeds. In attendance, a teeming swarm of maggoty vermin cleaned and rotated the spores, every pale mite diligently performing its assigned task.

Carefully, Sibatia gathered a handful of the tiny devils, slipping them into a small pouch tied to his belt. Taking his time, he began climbing the inner wall, scaling the girdling rings of fused vertebrae and bone. Halfway up, a frantic fist poked free and grabbed at his shorts, but he easily pried it loose and pulled himself through the orifice overhead.

Outside, a haze of floating pollen hovered above the Angel, stirred by the many fanlike ferns swaying gently upon its crown. Skirting an atrophied section of leathery putrefying flesh, doing his best to ignore the rank stench of decay and aging meat, Sibatia worked his way downward to the ground. Pausing to break off a gristly tidbit, he tossed it to Pudzo waiting patiently below.

203

True power is always heralded by great pain. Where the hell did he ever get that line from?

And that weird forest . . . Who exactly dreamed all that up?

Bidding the Angel farewell, Sibatia headed for Meru's shack, taking it nice and slow, walking with a noticeable bow-legged gait.

Seriously, now. He'd gone to find the girl and empty his balls, and instead her father comes out of nowhere and boots them?

Everything in this world is simple to understand, but when you get right down to it, nothing really makes any sense.

Running on ahead, Pudzo dashed into Meru's hut, and the girl inside immediately screamed. As Pudzo growled playfully, her boyfriend began squawking, that is until Sibatia stepped through the doorway and everyone shut up.

"Cut the guff," he told them. "Daddy's home."

Both of them had fallen from their chairs and were lying on the floor, semiparalyzed from the neck down. He must be losing his touch. By rights they shouldn't have been able to move so much as a hair for at least another two hours.

An energetic young couple, from the looks of it. But just how energetic remained to be seen.

"Time for another lesson, kids," he told them. Grasping the girl under her arms, he lifted her back into her chair, then gave Rolfe a hand as well.

Unfastening the felt bag from his belt, he dumped the vermin onto the table, enjoying the shocked expression on the girl's face as they formed into tight ranks and marched unerringly toward her, good little soldiers each and every one, scouts ranging wide on both flanks. From his large rawhide sack, Sibatia removed the rusty knife and pliers, setting them down with a solid clunk in the center of the table.

"Okay," he joked, "who's first?"

"What are you—" Rolfe muttered. "What are you going to do to us?"

Snatching up the knife, Sibatia sliced a line across the American's forehead, the blood instantly seeping down into his eyes. As he flopped and flailed and nearly fell to the floor again, the girl groaned with fear.

"You people," Sibatia said wearily. "Always so obsessed with what's going to happen. Appreciate the moment, boneheads. Glide."

Looking good and knowing it, little Anne began to cry. By now the doodlebugs had reached the table's edge and were swarming wildly in their eagerness to get at her.

"Do you know how crazy you are?" Sibatia asked. "You're always thinking. Always thinking. But a man of knowledge does not need to think."

Rising onto his tiptoes, he swiped the knife smoothly across the girl's brow, cutting her pallid American flesh.

"Listen, if you wish to learn the ways of the sorcerers, you have no more time for retreats or regrets."

He had their full attention now, at least for the moment. Setting the bloody knife down on the table, he pondered his next words carefully. There was so much he needed to teach them, so many things he wanted to share.

Where to begin?

"A true shaman," he tried, "never warms up his engines for longer or louder than necessary when he is getting off to an early start. Nor does he discard any trash that might float at sea, but keeps it in plastic containers to be disposed of on shore."

When he tore the girl's blouse open, she struggled briefly, with an animal desperation that pleased him on several levels. Reaching down, he fondled her sweet breasts with his inner hand, transfixing her heart.

"A true shaman, a warrior of the Old Ways, never speaks, rattles his clubs, or moves when another man of knowledge is making his shot." Grabbing the pliers, he struck Rolfe smartly on the bridge of his nose, silencing his annoying bleating. "You didn't know that, did you?"

Walking over to Meru's bed, Sibatia retrieved the bag of fresh seeds.

"A shaman never puts on airs when entertaining," he continued. From the corner near the window, Pudzo suddenly perked up and barked. "And of course, the same naturally goes for the shaman's dog."

One by one he counted out the lemon-size seeds for his American guests—seven each, he decided—ripe little suckers from the highest limbs.

Having abandoned Anne in order to gather around the bloody blade of the knife, the vermin now scrambled pell-mell for the nearest seeds, little sky-blue wormies tumbling all over one another, clicking and rustling, whispering their little wormy prayers.

"Following the circumcision ceremony," Sibatia continued, "a shaman consumes a joyful meal—often a brunch. The main course is never eaten with the fingers, however. You must cut off as much meat as you can—I mean this now—and leave the rest on your plate."

Moving to stand at Rolfe's side, Sibatia dabbed his thumb in the warm blood pooling freely from the wound in the American's forehead. He painted his own lips first, and then Rolfe's.

"When a man behaves in such a manner, one may rightfully say that he is a true warrior."

Picking up one of the seeds, brushing off the clinging vermin, Sibatia pressed it firmly against the American's mouth.

"Open wide now . . ."

CHAPTER FOURTEEN

1

He loved the way this story ended, with Demogoblin releasing the Living Darkness, Dr. Carnage meanwhile going, *Man is only the puniest of specks, a mere mite that has known sentience for but a nanosecond of galactic time.* And then that thing coming toward Earth from the other side of the universe, so huge it's blacking out like half the Milky Way.

"For my number four," Marshall said, "I think I'm gonna have to go with Mrs. Clinton."

"The President's wife?" Steve went. "Thou carcass fit for hounds!"

"Yeah, Steve, the President's wife is number four, and Chelsea's number three," Marshall said disgustedly. "You moron, I mean Mrs. Clinton, the third grade teacher."

"Oh, okay." Steve steered his flashlight around the ceiling of the lean-to. "Sure, she's pretty neat. I'll bet she could teach you a few things, too."

There is a festering tumor at the heart of every

galaxy, Dr. Carnage wails as he dies. *A dark cancer gnawing at the soul of every man.*

"My number three is . . . Bonnie Benge, all-time babe of babes."

Closing the comic, Howie switched off his flashlight. Bonnie Benge, everybody's favorite, by far the most beautiful girl in school. She was always high on everyone's list of Top Ten Foxes.

"Sorry, sheep-biter," Steve said. "She's all mine."

"My number two is, and just shut up, Doaks . . . Blossom."

Steve turned his flashlight off, and for a moment the lean-to was dark and quiet. "You mean, *the* Blossom?" he finally asked. "From TV?"

"It's that wild nose," Marshall confessed. "I can't help it. I watch her every week."

"If you're sick, my friend, see a doctor," Howie said.

"Hey, I like her too," went Steve. "Except in the middle of doing it, she'd probably jump up and start tap-dancing around the bed."

"Screw you guys, okay?" Marshall flicked his light on and off, and did a little fanfare trumpet kind of a deal with his mouth, same as Steve had done at the conclusion of his list. "And my number one fox of foxes . . . my ultimate megababe . . . is . . ."

"Your mom?" Howie guessed.

"Nancy Kerrigan," Marshall said. "America's sweetheart."

Lying in the silent darkness, Howie considered it, letting his imagination roam.

"Yeah, that smile, those awesome legs," Steve said respectfully. "Good choice, Kendall. I'm proud of you."

"Thanks."

"Don't mention it. Okay, How, your turn. Let's hear it."

"I'll stick with whatever I said last night." Howie sat up in his bunk, the metal frame squeaking loudly. "Listen, I say we get going. It's late enough."

"Ten fifty-eight," Marshall said, checking his watch. "If they were coming, they would've been here by now."

Because Steve and Howie had more or less personally been responsible for Troop 52's losing the game of Capture the Flag that evening, they had been expecting some kind of visit from Pinhead Doyle and Meathead McPherson. Apparently, though, their execution had been postponed until sometime tomorrow.

"Okay, let's go," Steve agreed, throwing off his blankets. "Who cares if they find out we're gone? We're dead anyway."

Already dressed, everyone climbed out of bed and put on their sneakers. Howie found his box of taffy and passed it around. With his new Swiss Army knife, Marshall cut his pieces in half so that they would last twice as long.

"Lighter, Howie?" Steve asked, holding up three Marlboros.

"Maybe we should leave a note for the Head Brothers," Marshall suggested.

"Neither of them can read," answered Howie. Lifting the corner of the front flap, he looked out into the night. The lean-tos on either side were dark, this whole section of the camp quiet and still. "Sleeping like babies," he said. "Dreaming away."

"Onward, bean-fed minions," said Steve, leading the way. "Thy bones are lacking marrow."

All kidding aside, they'd be in deep shit if they were caught, so they kept it down until they reached the baseball field. Pausing near second base, they lit their cigarettes, the crickets all around in the grass falling silent for a moment, waiting for them to pass on by. Overhead, thousands of stars hung above the valley, the Milky Way stretching clear and bright across the summer sky, rising over the edge of the world.

"How old do you think Blossom is?" Marshall asked.

"You mean like in real life?" said Steve.

"Yeah."

"Eighteen. Maybe nineteen."

"Oh," Marshall went.

Taking out his knife, he began flipping it into the ground, while Howie and Steve smoked and watched for shooting stars.

When you got right down to it, it was pretty obvious that all kinds of crap could be heading Earth's way. Meteors large enough to flatten Texas, freak cosmic rays capable of sterilizing the entire planet, rogue hordes of android assassins bent on exterminating any and all forms of organic life.

Floating around out in space the way it was, helpless and alone, the Earth wasn't much better off than a sitting duck on a shark-infested pond.

"Remember in *Close Encounters*," Howie said, "how that big ship at the end covered the whole sky?"

"Yeah, that was decent," Marshall agreed, the three of them all staring up at the stars now, smoking silently, the crickets coming alive to join the chorus of bullfrogs and peepers assembled down on the shore.

"How rich do you think she is?"

"Blossom?"

"Yeah."

"She's worth untold kerjillions," said Steve. "Come on, let's go."

In the darkness the lake looked at least twice its normal size. No more than half the cabins on the far side had their lights on. Flicking his cigarette into the water, Howie opened a taffy, picturing himself out there early Tuesday morning, swimming for his life, going for that mile merit badge.

What a way to die.

"Suppose nobody's there?" Marshall asked as they set out along the shore. "Suppose we get there and we don't find a thing?"

"You have something better to do?" Steve said, clicking his flashlight on right in Marshall's face, Marshall squinting like crazy, his hair sticking up all over the place. "If there's nothing going on, then we'll just turn around and come back."

"Where's your sense of adventure?" Howie went, snapping his flashlight on as well, a huge four-battery clunker that his dad had given him just for camp. "What would Blossom say?"

"Okay, okay," Marshall said. "I'm sorry I asked. Hold on a second, I have to take a wicked leak."

Standing at the water's edge, the three of them pissed together, ripples spreading out from shore across the star-filled sky.

"Remember, men," said Steve. "Aim low and fire in short, controlled bursts."

Suppose we do see something, though? Howie wondered, looking toward the lights on the opposite side of the lake. Then what?

A stretch of pine, a patch of swamp that cost Steve a soaker, and then a whole bunch of huge rocks and prickers. There was a path, sort of, but it still took them forever to reach the first cottage, which was dark and empty. After another thick batch of woods, a brook, and a second vacant cabin, they found themselves standing at last on the edge of an overgrown lawn, the RV parked right there in front of them.

Every light in the small house seemed to be on, but there wasn't a sound to be heard.

"Come on," Steve whispered after a moment, finally starting across the grass. "We can't wimp out now."

"Why not?" Marshall asked, still hesitating beside Howie. "Sure we can."

Halfway to the cottage Howie heard the first soft groans. Strange, panting, animal noises. He felt the skin on the back of his neck tighten as he exchanged glances with Marshall.

"Doaks, wait!" Marshall hissed, but Steve was already inching up to the side window, crouched low and keeping to the shadows.

There was another groan, louder this time, a strangled inhuman sound that nearly stopped Howie in his tracks. He reached the window two steps behind Marshall, and almost turned and ran when he saw the shocked expression on Steve's face.

"What?" he whispered. "What is it?"

Edging closer, he snuck a look into the window himself.

For a moment he couldn't understand what he was seeing. A terrible fear clouded his eyes.

There were people in there, naked people on the floor . . . all huddled together in a pile, all bleeding, with these spindly tubes lying all over them . . . green and yellow and blue tubes snapping like angry snakes . . .

And then Steve made a gagging sound, like he was about to puke, and one of the people jerked around and stared right at them, the cold wash of her gaze freezing Howie's heart, until suddenly he was running, following Steve, who was following Marshall, not back toward the woods but across the front lawn toward the road, Marshall racing under a tree in the middle of the yard now, straight into the arms of a dark figure dropping to the ground from the branches overhead.

2

The tree had become a great ship anchored to the Earth, straining under full sail to break free from its moorings, a thousand branches carding in the wind.

A living mast, a massive column of flesh, reaching toward the stars above—the Grandmother, the Sow, the Seven Angels. Closing her eyes and resting her cheek against the trunk, Molly could feel a gentle measured pulsing, the channels of warm sap rushing heavenward to quench the Red Ones' thirst.

Resuming her descent, she was nearly to the tree's base when she spotted the three boys coming across the lawn. Huffing and flailing, their young limbs loosened by panic, apparently they were fleeing for their little lives. Just as Molly was about to drop to the ground, the cottage door slammed open and Eddie stepped out onto the stoop.

"Get back here, you fucks!" he screamed.

Falling to the grass, Molly batted the first boy down,

punching him viciously in the throat. She grabbed the second kid by his hair as the third hesitated and then changed course, racing toward the trees to the left.

"Take these two inside," she called to Eddie.

She smashed the heel of her hand upward into the struggling boy's nose, splintering the cartilage easily. Flinging him to the ground beside his choking friend, she turned and went after the rabbit, the lizard skittering ahead of her across the grass, chattering excitedly.

Goddamn Boy Scouts.

Every summer it was the same deal. They were always snooping around, day and night, constantly bothering people on this side of the lake. Her father had often joked about installing some kind of megawatt Bug Buster in the backyard, something that would lure every last Scout out of the woods, zapping them all to a crisp, one by one.

At first the boy succeeded in eluding her, but not for long. The lizard eventually found him cowering beneath a thorn bush, and Molly was on him before he could slip free again, cracking his little Boy Scout head soundly against a boulder.

Carrying him back to the cottage, she gazed down at his youthful, innocent face, the flaccid tendrils on her breast uncurling to caress his narrow shoulders and chest.

Sweets for the sweet . . .

Inside, they were already working on the other two, Kim stripping the clothes off the kid with the crushed nose, while Eddie wrestled on the floor with the choking, wild-haired one.

"Can't breathe any better than a fish," he told

215

Molly, gesturing toward the thrashing boy beneath him. "Seems to me—correct me if I'm wrong—but I think you might've broken something."

Dropping the unconscious Scout in her arms onto the sofa, Molly watched the helpless child on the floor rise up and greet his Uncle. With his mouth twisted open around a silent scream and his eyes scrunched shut, he gagged and gasped until there wasn't any air left in his lungs, until his face seemed to finally relax and soften, his lips closing as his last breath was gently exhaled with a whispering sigh.

Well, maybe Uncle would build him a nice treehouse.

Tail eagerly aloft, turning mincing pirouettes around Kim and the second dying Scout, the lizard chirruped and piped its purling song. Busy fossicking about in Aileen's corpse, the little bicycle girl was lathering like a horse, the bunched cables and swollen bladders sprouting from her small frame slick with ejaculate and bloody discharge. Gabbling wordlessly in a shrill half whisper, Ben the dreadhead lay rocking beside her, the light jumping with some fathomless glee in his loony eyes.

"He hungers for the high life," Eddie said, giving the hippie a kick. "Some strange shit, eh, *compadre?*" he added, leaning over the gibbering man. *"Mondo bizarro."*

With a shimmy and a whuffing grunt, he straightened and grinned at Molly, showing his teeth as far back as his molars.

"Ai yi yi," he laughed, reaching up to coax a stubby rose-red tube from the opening below his navel. He raised his head like a dog sniffing the air. "The things we do for love."

Stepping forward, returning courtesy for courtesy, Molly eased into his embrace. She took him into her belly first, then parted her legs and swallowed him down there as well. A froth of mucous oozed from his breasts as he stretched in her strong arms, digging deeper into the warmth. She winced and smiled as he raked his nails along the bloody designs carved across her back, twisting against him to take him even further in.

He held her and helped her move, trembling like a leaf, both of them breathing hard, working themselves toward a little peace.

"When do we die?" he asked, eyes bright with a leaden heat.

Breaking free from inside a blister on his brow, a small white fly shook its wings and darted away.

"Never," she whispered. "Never."

There was a moment of softness then, bone on bone, as two crimson tears sluiced down her face. Body and soul, there was nothing left within her now but awe. She had lost the pull of time, the grip of gravity.

How could she keep from praising Him? He was so fearfully and wonderfully made, and all His works were marvelous.

Elated, she ascended toward the waiting light . . .

3

Things come around in all sorts of ways.

He tried not to be too surprised. Instead of getting a loop of wonder going in his heart, he tried to focus, to maintain his balance.

He tried to make no judgments about what he saw.

Returning from an indeterminate zone, he could feel his poor brain rubbing against his skull, rubbing itself smooth. A deep little tug, a slippery flux. Another edgy nudge from forces unknown.

Through half-opened eyes, particles of psychedelic brilliance darted beneath his lids.

Ah, vegetable bliss . . .

He had been gone so long this time, he'd kind of doubted he would ever make it back.

Holding up his arms, he calmly took note of the most recent developments, the fuzzy blue lumps running from his biceps to his hands, the delicate filigree of milky roots budding from the center of both palms.

Metagenesis, he thought. Now there's a righteous word.

Pivoting, he found Kim spraddled on the floor beside him, smiling raptly as she hugged the naked boy lying on her belly, his bloody face nestled between her breasts, his side torn open and swarming with a mass of jewel-headed worms. Eddie and Molly were right there as well, joined to one another by a tangled mesh of slender pipes and braided lengths of silvery cord, Eddie's hand embedded up to the wrist inside Molly's stomach.

218

God, the sort of things people can become, and so quickly too. It really was a revelation.

And hey, what's this? There was a second kid lying on the rug, and still another one up on the sofa.

But where the hell was Aileen?

Hearing a twitter behind him, a little-girl laugh all sunny and bright, Ben sat up and swiveled around, slowly, so as not to crimp the fragile cables encircling his waist.

He saw the lizard first, doing push-ups beside a small pile of black glass marbles, and then his eyes tracked left and he was looking at the blood-smeared girl, squatting on her heels right in the thick of Aileen, gulping air and laughing again as she rocked forward and buried her face in Aileen's remains, Aileen spread out all over the rug, everything percolating and astir, everything impossibly swollen and bloated, organs enlarged to the size of pillows, her entrails as fat as an uncoiled fire hose, twitching and waggling across the floor, the little girl sitting back now with Aileen's heart clutched in her hands, a pale red basketball studded with scores of dark barnaclelike knobs.

"You just relax," Eddie said to him, craning away from Molly, his face slick with sweat and pus. "Take it easy, you weedy sonovabitch."

Ben felt himself rising out of his head.

He tried to push himself onto his feet, but he couldn't do it, not even with the help of a chair. Heavy and numb, he sat panting for a few seconds, his thoughts scattering like an exploding star.

Lips peeled back, bad teeth clicking together, Eddie regarded him mockingly, his hands and groin busy with Molly.

"You tripped-out freak," he said. "Soon as I'm done

with this, I'm gonna lick you right down to the muscle. Then I'm gonna take your inflatable girlfriend and—"

There was nothing to it, really.

Reaching out, Ben grabbed a handful of Eddie and pulled, tearing free from his breast a swatch of crap like giant flabby ganglia, doughy snot-green stuff that reeked of fish.

Eddie's first reaction was amazement. Staring dreamily down at his wounded chest, he lifted a hand to cradle the half-dozen finger-sized slugs meandering around his right nipple.

"Don't worry," Ben said quietly, holding the junk up toward Eddie for his inspection. "It'll grow back."

And then the boy on the couch suddenly leapt up and lurched toward the door.

Good for you, kid, Ben thought. Good for you . . .

4

It was after midnight when he finally turned onto Lake Shore Drive.

He tried not to think of all the hours he'd lost, parked at that rest area, locked in some kind of terrible trance. He pushed the dreams from his mind, nightmares he knew he'd be reliving for the remainder of his life.

That madman in the crystal forest coming after him again and again, snarling with animal fury, teeth gnashing with a sound like grinding glass marbles . . .

As he passed Camp Keewaydin, he swerved to avoid a deer lying scattered across the road. Mind numb with dread, he counted the summer cottages slipping by, the lake sparkling through the trees in the moonlight.

What if the dreams never stop? he wondered. What if this is only the beginning?

Pulling into the driveway at last, he parked behind the RV and turned off the car, Harley jumping up in the seat and giving a little bark.

When the boy came flying through the front door, Charlie grabbed the rifle off the floor in back and climbed out, leaving Harley inside.

"Hey!" he called. "Over here!"

Staggering, the boy pitched forward to the ground before Charlie could reach him. Speechless with fear, he watched Charlie approach, his breath hitching in his chest as he pulled himself onto his knees.

"It's okay," Charlie told him. "Hey, it's okay."

But the kid wasn't listening. Wheeling around, he had his eyes fixed on the cabin as the screen door creaked open and somebody stepped outside.

"Christ All-fucking-mighty," said a loud raspy voice. "Now what?"

Charlie saw a figure standing on the shadowy front stoop, silhouetted against the light coming through the open door. Naked and gleaming, there were several thick ropes dangling around his waist. Half a dozen fat balloons quivered and shook on his stomach and chest.

"Come on in," he told Charlie amiably. "The more the merrier."

And then he was walking down the steps and onto the lawn, moving fast now, eyes glaring with inhuman malice as Charlie brought the rifle up, but not quickly enough, the guy easily swatting it aside, the balloons jiggling wildly as he grasped Charlie's throat.

"In the mood for some male bonding?" he asked, his hands like iron, forcing Charlie back, the ropes abruptly stiffening and wrapping themselves around Charlie's hips. "What's the matter, not your cup of meat?"

Struggling helplessly, Charlie dropped the rifle, desperately sucking in air. Somehow, he managed to wedge his left arm up in front of him, and groping blindly, he twisted one of the balloons until it squealed and burst, splashing his face with a warm gritty gel.

"You shit!" the guy shrieked, stumbling away, the ropes or hoses or whatever flailing slackly now against his legs. "Why the fuck did you do that?"

Falling to his knees, Charlie grabbed the rifle, swinging it up as Eddie came toward him.

"I'll shoot," he warned. "I swear to God I'll—"

And then Charlie fired, a split second after Eddie snatched the barrel and pushed it down, the gun discharging point-blank into his bare crotch.

With a pitiful wracking howl, Eddie reeled back, faltered, and then straight as a felled tree he toppled forward onto the grass, another two bladders exploding beneath him.

Dazedly crawling back onto his feet, gasping for air, Charlie heard the screen creaking once again. Spinning about, he saw someone holding the door open as something small darted down the steps, scuttling toward him across the lawn.

Quick as a spider, the lizard was on him, leaping onto his pants, its needle-sharp claws digging into his flesh as it frantically climbed upward.

Batting at the screeching creature with his fist, Charlie nearly knocked it away, but with a final flurry it slipped around onto his back and bit him on the side of the neck. Clinging there for a moment, it spat a mouthful of hot vomit into the wound, its little body pumping spastically, until at last it pulled off and jumped free, Charlie already feeling woozy, dropping down onto one knee, a dry, vacuous nausea sweeping over him in a long slow wave.

5

Standing near the driveway, Howie watched the old man with the rifle stumble and collapse, the lizard thing zigzagging around him on the grass, chirping and whistling like crazy. Behind Howie, inside the car, the man's dog was barking its head off, not at him but at the people coming out of the cabin now, all four of them shuffling down the steps at once, pressed together in a tight huddle.

Suddenly the man who had been shot began to scream, an endless warbling wail that echoed through the trees and out across the moonlit lake. Climbing slowly to his feet, he grabbed the rifle and started beating the old guy lying helplessly on the ground.

He's going to kill him, Howie told himself. And then he's going to come over here and kill me.

Whirling around, his legs nearly buckling beneath him, Howie turned toward the road.

"That's right, junior," Eddie called after him, grunting as he swung the rifle. "Go ahead and run. I'll be with you in a minute."

The first door Howie tried was locked, but then the driver's door opened and the big German shepherd

223

came flying out, fur bristling, knocking him down as it charged past. By the time Howie pulled himself up against the car, the dog had already reached Eddie.

Leaping onto him, snapping its massive jaws, it shook its head savagely from side to side, tearing at the plump cords and dangling bladders.

It was over within a matter of moments.

Tugging with all its might, the dog growled and reared back, coming away with a whole cluster of stuff. Eddie immediately went down with a short groan of dismay, his wide-open belly all wet and shiny.

Howie felt his stomach turning over at the sight. Weak and rocky, fear choking his throat, he leaned against the car, his head throbbing painfully with every pulse of his heart.

With dreamlike slowness the people standing near the cabin started walking across the lawn—the two women, the man, and the young girl—shoulder to shoulder, feet moving together with an awkward crabbing motion. Glancing briefly toward Howie, the girl gave him a bright feral smile.

Reaching the old man lying on the ground, they paused as one of the women stepped forward, a trailing spray of hanging cables connecting her to the group. Holding out a hand, she said something to the dog, who was now standing guard beside the man, snarling menacingly.

"Harley?" she went. "Hey, boy, it's me."

When she moved closer, though, the dog barked wildly, feigning a charge.

Retreating back into the waiting arms of the others, the woman studied the unconscious old man for several moments, as if trying to determine how badly he might be hurt.

And then, as Howie finally turned and fled, staggering down the dark road toward the camp, the little girl led everyone over to the tree in the middle of the yard, where they all stretched out on top of one another in a pile.

6

How simple and strange everything is . . .

When she was very young, three or four years old, her father loved to give her rides on his shoulders.

Get up here, he'd laugh, taking her by the arms and holding her up to the sun. *Here we go.*

She could still hear his voice, even now. Exactly the way it sounded then. She'd be high off the ground, but she wouldn't be afraid, because they were holding onto each other. Moving across the yard, she would keep her hands tight around his forehead.

You can let go now, he'd say, gripping her ankles. *I've got you, honey.*

When he said that, it wasn't as if he just thought it, it was as if he was announcing some truth, some truth she always believed.

Okay, he'd say. *You're flying now.*

I've got you, honey. You won't fall.

Holding her arms out on either side, she rode up high on his shoulders, up near the trees.

She could still hear his voice, even now as she was dying.

Don't you worry, Molly.

Here we go . . .

7

Fifteen minutes? Thirty? After a timeless time, Charlie awoke. Aching and ill, he slowly sat up and looked around.

The man he had shot was still sprawled on the ground, but nowhere near where he'd been before. And the boy was gone, hopefully having escaped unharmed.

When Charlie noticed the thing under the maple tree, resting against the trunk, at first he thought this was another dream.

But no.

No, this was real. There were legs and faces in the cushiony mass, people's bleared faces and bones.

"Harley, get away from there," he called out, forcing himself to stand and limp unsteadily across the lawn.

Made of brittle blue twigs, a rickety branching structure rose from the bloody mound, creepers reaching up and clinging to the trunk of the tree. Glancing higher, Charlie saw the lizard waiting on a limb overhead.

It peered down at him for a long moment, studying him carefully, before finally turning and scurrying off, climbing toward a faint glow shimmering above, the tree trembling now as if stirred by a gentle wind . . . a wind born half a world away.

"Daddy, I'm afraid," the mass of flesh and bone whispered, one face surfacing now, Molly's face, bloated ivory eyes swiveling around with a sickening squelchy sound.

"Daddy?"

A berserk grimace swept over her distorted features as her blind gaze locked onto his. It was an expression from which all humanness had vanished. Her hairless skull seemed to bulge outward, and a dozen small dark spheres slipped from her mouth, rolling onto the grass.

"Daddy?"

Turning away at last, Charlie searched for his rifle. He would never awaken, not from this dream. That much he knew.

CHAPTER FIFTEEN

~~

There are angels who have no form at all, but come as pure, raw energy," he told the American. "Great sweeping balls of fire, like supernovas, circling in deepest space. They are called Wheels or Thrones."

Yanking the boy's head back, Sibatia slid another seed home—five down, two to go—Rolfe gagging weakly, his strength nearly gone.

"Remember," Sibatia said, clamping Rolfe's jaw shut. "Just as dough cannot be made to rise without a ferment, so flesh must be sublimed and purified. Swallow, you little shit . . . There, that's better."

Giving Rolfe a pat on the head, he reached for the next seed.

Sitting on Meru's bed, Tembro chuckled, grinning like a hound. Resting in his arms, the baby squirmed fitfully, its face seamlessly fused to his chest. Outside the hut, Pudzo was halfheartedly barking at something, his voice fading as he wandered off into the trees.

"Listen," Sibatia said, cramming the sixth seed down the white boy's gullet. "Part animal, part djinn,

228

Auntie Spikes has great charm. I say this in all sincerity. Not only is her womb a haven of delight, it also serves as a place of terror and destruction."

Picking up the final seed, Sibatia cradled it in his hands for a moment, admiring its delicate beauty.

"My dear little monkey, don't you recognize the most self-evident fact?" With considerable gentleness, he pushed the last seed in, patiently stroking Rolfe's throat. "It is an extremely painful thing to be ruled by laws that one does not understand."

Blah, blah, blah . . .

Sometimes, he wondered why he bothered.

"Okay, you're next, sunshine," he said, turning to the girl sitting across the table.

Brushing the vermin off her first seed, Sibatia studied her as she struggled against the invisible fetters securing her to the chair. On the table before her, six additional seeds were arranged alongside the ritual knife and pliers.

"I don't see why you're being so difficult about this," he said, reaching out to tenderly caress her exposed breasts. "You shouldn't take it so personally."

Stepping back, he slipped the seed into his own mouth and quickly swallowed it down. "See, nothing to it."

Coughing it up, he held the black ball directly in front of her face. "Your trouble is, you have no romance in your soul. And frankly, that's an attitude I don't wish to encourage."

Grasping her hair firmly, he leaned forward and placed the seed against her lips.

"A true warrior has nothing to fear from the—"

229

The pain was so intense and sudden, he didn't really feel it at first. Looking down, he saw the ritual knife sticking out of his belly.

With a muted grunt, the girl jerked her hand upward once again, burying the blade all the way to the handle.

The unknown, he thought, as the girl pulled the knife free and he crashed to the floor.

A true warrior has nothing to fear from the unknown.

With only mild interest Sibatia watched Tembro walk over, take the knife from the girl, and slit her throat.

Then he must've blacked out for a while, because suddenly he was in Tembro's arms, being carried through the sacred grove. Squeezed against his shoulder, the baby's bare back was clammy and cold.

When they reached the black gum tree, Tembro bent down and dropped Sibatia to the ground, the shock knocking the air from his lungs. Rising above him, the Angel rested in the shade.

As the ring of velvety orifices made soft propulsive sounds of greeting, bulging seed pods dispersed plumes of gold and white confetti. Pallid tendrils unreeled to tickle and probe him, their tiny beaklike barbs prickling his skin.

"Tembro," he said, giving a long shuddering sigh. "Tembro . . . move me closer."

One by one the seconds passed. A column of foraging vermin paraded out from the Angel, gamboling like little drunken men when they happened upon Sibatia's blood.

"Tembro," he tried again. "I . . . I need to go inside Her."

Subtly, everything changed. Colors fluctuated ever

so slightly, and the outlines of objects sharpened. There was some kind of disturbance in the air, a flickery brightness settling around him. It was as if a cloud had passed from the sun.

Levering himself onto his back, Sibatia caught a trace of motion high in the gum tree overhead. All fish-eyed and gawping, his tongue darting in and out of his red mouth, Tembro stared upward and giggled.

His heart fluttering in his chest, Sibatia watched the lizard's rapid scrabbling descent, thinking, *Why has it returned so soon?* Thinking, *Something must've gone wrong.*

My True Western Bride, what has happened to you? My lovely . . .

With a frightened squeak, Tembro turned and shuffled off, fleeing into the trees.

Naked and erect, jet-black and skeletally thin, Uncle Dry Skull ambled out from behind the Angel. He glanced down at Sibatia for a moment, regarding him blandly. Skinned and eviscerated, Pudzo dangled from a rawhide cord around his waist.

"The fuck is this mess?" he finally asked, gesturing toward the Angel, a twinge of exasperation in his voice.

"I . . ." Sibatia expelled a quavering breath. "I just want . . ."

"What, little man?" Uncle said. "Come on, tell me. What do you want?"

"America," Sibatia said quietly. "I just wanted to see America."

Uncle's laughter was bitter and sharp. Looking up at the Angel, his faraway eyes went bright with amusement.

"America? Are you shitting me? America?" Rising

above Sibatia, his body glinted in the sunlight, teeth clicking softly. "Okay, *mganga*. Whatever you say . . . But hey, look here."

Bending down until his face filled the sky, Uncle opened his mouth wide, and then wider still, his jaw ratcheting back like a snake's. Inch by inch the mouth moved lower.

Were those really stars in there? Yes, Sibatia could see them.

Soon, they were everywhere.

"Come on, little man," Uncle's voice said inside his head. "Time to fly."

The world was drifting slowly away, sloughed off like an old skin.

"Time to fly," the voice repeated. "Time to fly."

A true warrior has nothing to fear from the unknown, right?

Screaming, Sibatia ascended into the waiting darkness.